LOW
LIFE

Also by Ryan David Jahn

Acts of Violence

LOW LIFE

RYAN DAVID JAHN

MACMILLAN

First published 2010 by Macmillan
an imprint of Pan Macmillan, a division of Macmillan Publishers Limited
Pan Macmillan, 20 New Wharf Road, London N1 9RR
Basingstoke and Oxford
Associated companies throughout the world
www.panmacmillan.com

ISBN 978-0-230-74682-4

1 3 5 7 9 8 6 4 2

A CIP catalogue record for this book is available from
the British Library.

Typeset by Intype Libra, London
Printed and bound in the UK by CPI Mackays, Chatham ME5 8TD

For Dave Morton and Jacque Morton –

who bought me my first typewriter

Thanks to

Will Atkins
Liz Cowen
Gordy Hoffman
Mary Jahn
Andy Pagana
Sophie Portas
Heather Schor

1

SIMON

The morning of the day Simon first killed a man felt completely ordinary.

He was lying on a ratty twin-size mattress, which was resting directly upon a nail-riddled hardwood floor. An alarm clock, his glasses, and an orange prescription-pill bottle sat on the floor nearby. The only other piece of furniture in the room was a dresser which looked like it should have been left curbside years ago. Simon was flat on his back, arms at his sides, covered in a thin brown blanket. By all appearances he was asleep, face calm and relaxed. His cheeks were pale and littered with old acne scars. Erase the eyes and the nose and the mouth and you could have been looking at the surface of the moon, or perhaps some remote atomic test site. His hair was prematurely gray – he was thirty-four but had the thin, whitish, brittle hair of an eighty-year-old – and very choppy, despite the fact that he carefully parted it on the right and combed it down slick with pomade. He cut it himself. He hated barbers. When he used to go he always felt a captive of this man with a weapon, forced to listen to inanities concerning the day-to-day life of a person about whom he gave not a solitary shit, and, worse, forced to answer inquiries about his own life.

Simon was not one for small talk.

He opened his eyes.

A gray light was seeping in around the edges of a blue curtain which was really no curtain at all; it was a blanket purchased from a street vendor and nailed over the window with the use of a coffee mug. Simon kept waiting for his porcelain hammer to shatter while he banged away but it never did.

Am I awake?

He blinked.

I must be awake, he thought. Everything makes sense.

His alarm clock made a hollow click. A moment later it sounded.

He sat up, the blanket falling off his chest. The morning air was cool, despite the fact that it was late summer. He wasn't sure of the exact date; each day was so like the one that came before it that days and dates didn't seem to matter. He could tell you how many steps it took to get from the elevator at work to his cubicle – seventy-four if he was in a good mood, eighty-two if he was feeling low – but he couldn't tell you the date. It was early in the morning and the room was night-chilled despite the fact that it was late summer. That was all.

Or maybe it was early fall. He was pretty sure it was September, anyway.

He grabbed the alarm clock, silenced it, and then gave it back to the floor. He picked up his glasses, metal-framed aviator-type jobs with thick lenses that shrunk his eyes by half – he was near-sighted – and set them on the bridge of his nose. He cringed as he did so and sucked in air with a hiss. Despite the fact that he had needed glasses since he was ten, and this pair was not new, over the last several weeks he had developed a sore behind his right ear from the plastic earpiece digging into his flesh. It was raw and rather bloody. When he touched the pad of a finger against the wound it stung sharply. He had tried to bend and contort the glasses into a more comfortable shape but the attempt proved futile.

Simon got to his feet. The hardwood floor was cold. He had gone to bed wearing socks but at some point in the night must have pulled them off because they were now lying inside-out on the floor in the corner of the room like dead rodents.

In a T-shirt and green checkered pajama bottoms he stood over the dirty blue basin in his bathroom, water slowly drip-drip-dripping from the leaky faucet. He looked at himself in the surface of the medicine cabinet's toothpaste-spotted mirror. The reflective film on the other side of the glass was peeling away like sunburned skin, revealing the tubes and bottles of salves and pills inside. Simon moved the hard bristles of his toothbrush across the bony surface of his teeth. His gums hurt and when he spit into the basin there was a swirl of red mixed in with the toothpaste white. He turned on the water and rinsed it away.

After a luke-warm shower – the water never got hot – he slipped into boxers, a pair of brown pants, and a white shirt. He wrapped a tattered paisley tie, light blue pattern on a brown background, around his neck and slipped into a brown corduroy sport coat with leather elbow patches. He put on socks with holes in them and a pair of brown suede shoes which were old and stained, the suede flat and slick with age and use, the thin leather laces snapped and tied together again in multiple places.

He walked to the kitchen, where he made himself two liverwurst sandwiches with white onion and swiss cheese, packed two pickles and a handful of potato chips in cling wrap, wrapping them individually, and packed it all into a brown paper bag which he folded twice at the top, along creases already present from prior use.

That done, he looked at his watch – it was seven-thirty, work started at eight – and headed for the front door.

Once through it, he turned around and shoved a key into the scratched and loosely fitted brass lock and tried to twist the deadbolt home. Whoever had installed the lock, however, had done a poor job of it and the deadbolt and the slot into which it was supposed to slide did not line up. Simon had to lift up the doorknob with one hand and rattle it while simultaneously turning the key in order to get the job done. Finally, after some under-the-breath cursing – come on, you son of a bitch – the lock slid home.

The corridor floor was covered with a carpet that might once have been beige but which was now leopard-spotted with stains and trampled flat where it wasn't in tatters. The edges where a vacuum couldn't reach and the center where most of the walking took place were solid black. The walls were nicotine yellow except where graffiti had recently been painted over, and despite the freshly painted-over spots that littered them there was also a new graffito, no more than two days old. It was on the wall opposite the stairwell that led down to the perpetually unattended lobby at street level.

WELL, TAKE HIM

it read. It had been spray-painted on, the nozzle held close to the wall. Surrounding the lettering were several splatter spots, and runs dripping down from it. Above was a finger-painted 's'. Simon assumed that whoever had done the painting had accidentally held his finger in the way of the nozzle's flow, hadn't liked the result on the pad of his index, and had attempted to wipe it onto the wall.

Well, take him. Take whom? Take him where?

Simon walked toward the graffito, turned his back to it, making a mental note to call his landlord, Leonard, and let him know about it (he wouldn't be happy: he just painted over another graffito in the same spot only a few days ago), and headed down a creaky flight of stairs not quite wide enough for two people walking in opposite directions to pass without brushing against one another. The lightbulb overhead had burned out a couple of months earlier and still hadn't been replaced, so even now, while a bright morning shone outside, it was night-time in the stairwell. As he walked down the wooden steps, listening to them issue moaning complaints at his weight, he smelled the familiar stench of urine. The lobby's front door was kept unlocked, which resulted in the place being graffitied, as well as the occasional bum sleeping in the stairwell.

At the bottom of the stairs, the lobby. It might have reeked of charm ninety-five years ago when the building was constructed, but now it was possessed by the stench of decay. The tile floor was cracked and stained, the grout either blackened with filth or altogether missing; the wainscoting warped and scarred with carved initials; the windows foggy with filth; the slowly rotating fan blades hanging from the ceiling lined with an inch of dust they'd spent decades cutting through, dust which occasionally grew too heavy to hold its grip and dropped in great gray chunks like dead pigeons.

Simon walked through this, and then pushed his way out of the fingerprinted glass doors and onto Wilshire Boulevard, where the Filboyd Apartments stood, one of the city's many growths, rising twelve storeys into Los Angeles's sun-bleached sky, rectangular and utilitarian as a barrack, a rusted fire escape etching a crooked spine down its back. Immediately the sounds and smells of the city accosted him – diner food and exhaust fumes, car horns and helicopters.

Half a block away, a bum was sleeping on a bench in front of a restaurant called Captain Bligh's (which sold an impossible-to-finish one-pound Bounty Burger). Traffic flowed like a steel river along Wilshire, dammed at various intersections and slowed to a trickle here and there. Across the traffic-filled street, a low strip of buildings – an electronics store, a laundromat, a Korean barbecue place.

Simon turned right on the sidewalk and started west on Wilshire to find his car. He was about halfway there when he saw the dog. It was a mangy thing with reddish-brown fur and a left ear that looked like a piece of steak fat that had been chewed on a while. Its fur was matted with blood and filth. Its right eye was pure white with blindness but for a red vein bulging in one corner.

Simon paused mid-stride.

He looked at the dog and the dog, which had simply been limping along to who knew where, stopped and looked back. Its good eye was bright and alive and sad all at once. Something about the thing broke Simon's heart.

He sat on his haunches and set his lunch bag between his feet. He opened the top and dug inside, pulling out one of the liverwurst sandwiches from beneath pickle spears which were already leaking through their wrappers. He peeled the sandwich and held it out to the dog.

'Come here, boy.'

The mutt cocked its head to the left, looking at Simon.

'Come on, it's liverwurst.'

The mutt took a few hesitant steps toward him, walking sidewise, as if afraid of coming at him straight, its yellow nails clicking against the pavement. Once it was within about a foot of Simon's outstretched arm, it stopped and looked over its shoulder, guilt in its eye, afraid it was doing something that would earn it a swift kick from some unseen punisher. Then it stretched its neck toward the sandwich, grabbed it in its jaw, and scampered several feet away before dropping it to the sidewalk and eating it in a few quick bites.

'That was nice of you.' A thin, reedy voice.

Simon stood up – a brief dizziness swimming over him, black dots dancing before his eyes – and turned around to see an old man – at least ninety, maybe older – whose faced was lined with wrinkles, who had parentheses stacked up on either side of his mouth. Loose skin sagged from his neck and the bags under his eyes looked capable of holding a pint apiece. His lips were colorless. He wore a moth-eaten yellow cardigan and a pair of well-ironed – though threadbare – slacks and polished leather shoes that he'd probably owned since leaving Germany in 1956, or whenever it had been. The accent was thin but still easily detectable. He looked at Simon with eyes that were pale blue and raw.

Simon said, 'Thank you,' and then broke eye contact.

The old man nodded but didn't move and didn't speak. His gaze was steady.

Simon felt as if the old man expected something from him.

'I have to get to work.'

The old man nodded again but remained silent.

'Okay,' Simon said. 'Have a good day.'

He turned around and walked away. He glanced over his shoulder once before reaching his old Volvo, and then got into it, made an illegal u-turn – quickly, while traffic was blocked on either side by red lights – and drove toward downtown, where a pack of buildings jutted from the horizon like crooked teeth.

He spent his morning crunching numbers. He worked for a large payroll company that occupied the twentieth floor of a building whose main purpose seemed to be blotting out the sun. He sat in his black chair at his brown desk inside his gray cubicle and punched away at the number pad on his white keyboard.

*

When lunchtime arrived he got up from his desk, grabbed his lunch bag from the office fridge – which stunk of the rotten food that had gotten pushed to the back – walked down the hallway to the elevator, and waited. The building was fifty storeys tall and had an elevator for every ten-floor section, one through ten, eleven through twenty, twenty-one through thirty, and so on, each one stopping at the lobby level for pick-up and drop-off. The elevator came and went and the people standing with him got onto it and went away – and he continued to wait. After several minutes an empty elevator arrived and there was no one left waiting but him. He stepped onto it, knowing he was foolish to wait for the solitude of an empty elevator when it would certainly be full by the time he reached the lobby, but having to do it anyway.

The elevator stopped on the seventeenth floor and picked up two women.

He turned to the brushed-steel corner of the elevator and closed his eyes. They stung and he pinched them tighter. His chest felt cramped somehow. He tilted his head up toward the fluorescent lights in the ceiling and the black cover of his eyelids went red.

'. . . and then Vince says, "What do I care who you sleep with?"'

'Unbelievable.'

'I know, right?'

'What did you do?'

'I told him I slept with his brother.'

'Did you?'

'No. Vince's brother smells like a dumpster. I just wanted to see how he'd react.'

'And?'

On the fifteenth floor several others joined the party – and on the twelfth and eleventh.

By the time he reached the lobby, Simon felt sweaty and hot and slightly sick; the elevator was packed with people.

He rushed out of it, pushing past several slowpokes – hearing a 'Hey, buddy' and an 'Asshole' as he did so – and swiftly made his way through the marble-floored lobby to the non-recycled air and daylight of the outside world. He was breathing hard. He felt stupid for panicking over a crowded elevator, but he didn't know how not to panic over it. Yet twenty floors was a lot of walking. So he simply took the elevator and felt sick four times a day – once in the morning; twice at lunchtime, once down and once up; and once when the day was over.

He blinked in the noontime light, his pupils shrinking to pinpoints. Robert and Chris were both standing in front of the building, smoking cigarettes.

Robert was tall and thin, wore suits that hung on his bony body like trash bags, and had a ponytail hanging off the back of his head that looked like a horse's tail. He had a weak chin and a large forehead, which in an earlier age might have marked him as some sort of degenerate, and surprisingly small and delicate hands for a man his height.

Chris was about five three, a stringy little Texan with teeth like rotting fence posts and thin blond hair combed straight down onto his forehead. His face seemed somehow too large for the head it had been slapped onto, big eyes like a lemur, and a wide fish mouth. The muscles behind the flesh often twitched for no apparent reason, especially when he got on a rant, which was frequently.

Simon had no idea how old either of them was – maybe thirty-five, maybe forty.

Robert looked at his watch. 'You finally give up and start taking the stairs?'

Simon smiled a smile that felt forced and false. His eyes felt dull in his head.

Even though he considered Robert and Chris his friends – his only friends, really – he did not know how to react to them. He felt lost in the world of human interaction. He thought that after thirty-four years of life he sometimes knew what was expected of him in social situations – he had learned the correct reactions through trial and error – but it never felt natural. It felt like a performance. He was supposed to smile so he smiled. He was supposed to laugh at a joke so he laughed. He was supposed to talk to his friends about television programs so he watched television in order to have something to talk about. But he felt apart from it – separated from it by some invisible membrane, stuck outside even himself, in some no-place, watching himself interact with the world from a distance – unable to join in, even while he appeared to be doing so.

They headed to a place called Wally's on Broadway and grabbed a table. Robert and Chris ordered their lunches. Simon sat and waited for their sandwiches to arrive before unpacking his own. When he first began eating his lunches here with Robert and Chris – four months ago, three months after he started working in the same building with them, though it felt like he'd been working here forever: every day was the same and they seemed to stack infinitely into his past like a line of dominoes – there was some trouble with the manager. This was a restaurant, not a park. He couldn't just bring his own food in here and spread out. But since then they'd worked it out, and the manager let it slide.

When Babette brought out Simon's daily 7-Up, she smiled and said hello. Simon returned the smile, pulled the paper sleeve off the top of his straw, and took a draw. It was cold and sweet and helped to settle his stomach.

He fell into his car, the work day over. The car was a gray 1987 Volvo. The paint was peeling from the hood where the heat of the engine had cooked it and from the trunk where several different owners had set the gas cap when refilling the tank. He started the engine, thumbed the button on the left of the transmission's handle, and dragged it down to drive. He pulled out into the slow flow of traffic, edging in with his right fender – this was a one-way street – forcing the car behind him either to stop or hit him. Take your pick, pal. In five minutes he was back on Wilshire and heading toward home. But then he drove right past the Filboyd Apartments and past the Ambassador Hotel, where Robert Kennedy was assassinated forty years earlier, and onward. The Ambassador was under construction, being turned into a school, its history knocked away with the walls, goodbye Cocoanut Grove, hello detention, and there was nothing left of it but its steel skeleton surrounded by great pits of earth and a chain-link fence. Los Angeles was a city that perpetually razed its own past. History was for people who hadn't yet made it here. This was the edge of the new world and it would remain so. You couldn't go any further, and who would want to? Just ignore the slums and the dirt and the poor and try not to trip over any broken dreams while walking down Hollywood Boulevard.

In another few miles he reached his destination. The front of the place simply read

ADULT BOOKS & VIDEO ARCADE

and though he had never seen an actual book inside, there were certainly plenty of magazines.

He parked his car on a side street just off Wilshire, checked the meter, found that whoever had parked there last had left him twenty-three minutes of free parking, added a quarter's worth of time, and then walked along the cracked sidewalk toward the arcade.

The metal gate which acted as a front door was locked. It was always locked. Simon pressed a button on the wall to his right and heard a bell chime inside. He looked up at the camera mounted above the door. A moment later, a buzzing sound. Simon pulled on the door. It opened.

The place was humid and smelled of ocean salt and rotting undersea vegetation or – more likely – of something that resembled those combined odors; it was fifteen miles to the nearest beach in Santa Monica, where a Ferris wheel spun slowly and bikinied women lay on brightly colored towels, and the only seabirds this far inland were gulls hanging out behind the seafood restaurant on Fourth and Vermont, picking through the shrimp shells and lobster tails left in its dumpster.

At the counter – behind which stood a bored-looking fellow in a burgundy tracksuit, who was flipping through a wrestling magazine – Simon exchanged a twenty-dollar bill for twenty one-dollar bills, and then made his way through the front room, where rows of magazine covers displayed various fetishes – close-ups of well-manicured feet with red and blue polished toenails; the tiny breasts, puffy nipples and bald vaginas of women pretending to be prepubescent girls; submissive women whose waists were cinched by corsets and whose asses were welted red by thorough canings; nurses wielding enema nozzles; pigtailed women in diapers tonguing pacifiers – and then through a doorway and up a single step into the back room above whose door was a sign which labeled it the

VIDEO ARCADE

A few lonesome middle-aged men with glistening black eyes were hanging around outside the booths, apparently looking to find someone with whom to share some of their time inside before heading home to their wives (Simon saw several wedding bands). He avoided eye contact, not wanting to give anyone the wrong idea, and made his way to a booth with a green light glowing above it. The booths with red lights above them were occupied, their doors locked, and the faint sounds of videotaped sex issued from the cracks beneath their doors.

There was a television built into one of the walls inside the booth, and to its right a slot for collecting dollar bills. On the wall opposite the television, a built-in wood bench. On the floor beside it, a trash can half-filled with wadded-up kleenexes and paper towels and fast-food napkins. The stench of rotting ectoplasm was overwhelming.

Simon put a dollar bill into the slot beside the television, and the screen came aglow, filling the small room with sickly light.

The television displayed six channels of pornography, which came in six distinct flavors. Simon chose channel three – a woman in a black leather mask was flogging a completely nude man, who was on hands and knees on a cracked concrete floor in some anonymous warehouse (probably a warehouse just over the hill in Sherman Oaks or Encino). She called him terrible names while she beat him.

Simon did not sit down, but his knees felt shaky.

When he got back to the Filboyd Apartments he could not find parking on Wilshire, so he turned left onto a side street lined with apartment buildings and drove north toward Sixth. Near the end of the block, beneath a broken streetlamp – all of the lamps were out on this block, while across Sixth they were turning on in the dim evening light – he found a spot he could barely squeeze his car into, and proceeded to do so, his right front fender poking only slightly into a red zone. A fire plug jutted from a brown patch of grass about ten feet away.

He stepped from the Volvo, slammed the door shut, put his key into the scratched-up keyhole, and gave it a turn from twelve to three. There was a satisfying resistance, and then all four doors locked simultaneously with a chorus of thwacks. He turned away from the car and started south toward home, stuffing keys into his pocket.

Both the sun and the moon were visible as they changed shifts, the moon high and the sun sinking below the horizon. The clouds looked like pulled cotton. The nearest stars – or perhaps they were planets – poked through the darkening sky like flashlights in a distant wood.

A few steps from his car he stopped to light a cigarette. After getting it lighted, he flipped the cap over the silver Zippo, snuffing the flame, and stuck it warm into his pants pocket. He could feel the heat of it against his thigh. He took a drag and felt the smoke swirling within his lungs, heavy and hot and somehow comforting. He exhaled through his nostrils. His father – adoptive: Simon didn't know who his birth parents were, though in his youth he had often made up different stories about them, and about why they dumped him off at an Austin, Texas, police station when he was only three months old – used to smoke Camel Filters and often exhaled through his nostrils. When he was a small boy he thought it was the coolest thing in the world, how someone could take smoke into his mouth and exhale it through his nose. It seemed like it must be some kind of magic.

He continued walking south. He made it only seven steps before something terrible happened.

It began with someone saying, 'You got the time?' But not to him. The voice came from across the street. Simon looked over there and saw a tall guy with a neck tattoo standing only a couple of feet from an old man wearing a moth-eaten yellow cardigan.

'Let me see,' the old man said. He had a German accent, his voice thin and reedy.

He pushed back the left sleeve of his cardigan, revealing a silver watch which glistened in what was left of the light. He squinted at the numbers, pulling his head away from his own outstretched arm, apparently far-sighted and without his glasses.

'I think it's about—'

Two other men stepped out of the shadows of a brick apartment building – one with a Dodgers cap on his head, the other's bald pate slick as a polished bowling ball – grabbed the old man's arms from behind and started pounding at his kidneys. He cried out once or twice, but then his breath must have been gone because after that all he managed were sad little grunts. His legs gave, knees buckling, but the other men held him up and continued to punch at him for a while, his feet dragging on the concrete beneath him as he was punched and jostled, making quiet scuffling sounds like whispers. Then they emptied his pockets of a billfold, removed his watch, and let him crumple to the sidewalk, let him simply fold on top of himself. The guy with the neck tattoo gave him three more kicks to the gut, and then said to one of the others, 'Get his shoes. I can wear 'em to church.'

'Get 'em yourself if you want 'em. They're not my size.'

The guy with the neck tattoo cursed, 'Lazy bastard,' and then pulled the shoes off the old man's feet, revealing plaid yellow socks that matched the cardigan.

'Hey,' Simon said, after snapping out of his stunned silence. 'What are you guys doing?'

But they weren't doing anything. They'd finished.

'You want some too?' the bald one said.

'No, thank you.'

'Forget about him,' said the one with the neck tattoo.

'It can be a two-for-one night.'

'No. Fuck him. I'm hungry. Let's get a taco.'

'You lucked out this time, fucker!'

They turned and walked away from there. Simon stood motionless a moment or two longer – wanting to make sure they weren't going to return – and then jogged across the street to where the old man lay motionless.

He knelt down – cigarette dangling from his dry lips, smoke wafting into his eyes, making them water – and felt for a pulse. He felt nothing. If ever a pulse had been there, it was in the wind now. The old man was dead.

When he reached Wilshire he found a pay phone, a small metal box set against a brick wall, and called the police. He did not want to call from his home telephone because he did not want the police to show up and question him for hours about something that had lasted thirty seconds. He told the woman who answered that he had witnessed a mugging. Three men had accosted an old man with a German accent. He told her where it had happened and described the three men as well as he could given the distance and the dim light. He told her that the old man was dead. When the woman asked him his name he simply hung up and walked away.

*

He walked through the empty lobby and up the creaky stairs and across the leopard-spotted corridor floor to his apartment. He could hear the Korean couple four doors down yelling at each other (though he couldn't understand them), and somewhere else nearby someone was watching a situation comedy which kept spitting out laugh track ha-has that sounded like a lawnmower trying to start. He unlocked the front door and stepped inside. Before closing the door behind him – before locking out the forty-watt light coming in from the naked bulbs in the corridor ceiling (the fixtures long since shattered or stolen) – he fumbled around in the dark for the switch on the inside wall, found it, flipped it, and with a *click* the old yellow lamp with its crooked and stained paper shade came to life, lighting up the glossy covers of a few paperback novels, with which it shared an end table, as well as the rest of the room. Then he closed the door, set the deadbolt, and slid the chain into place.

The living room was about twice the size of the bedroom. The walls were stained yellow and white patches where the last tenant had hung pictures were still visible, rectangular evidence that someone else had once lived here. Every time someone in the building flushed a toilet or washed their dishes the rusty pipes behind the walls shook and rattled and moaned with ghostly voices. The brown and red striped couch sagged in the middle and horsehair stuffing poured from holes in the fabric. The coffee table which sat in front of it was made of pressboard and the thin sheet of imitation wood which covered it was peeling at the corners and chipping away. On top of the coffee table, a Mason jar filled with water in which a goldfish swam.

'Hello, Francine. How you doing?'

He sprinkled flakes of fish food onto the water where they formed a thin scrim on its surface. Francine opened her little black mouth and sucked in bits of it. He stood and watched her eat in silence for a couple minutes and then headed into the kitchen to fix himself dinner.

The whiskey was good and strong and cold on top of the ice cubes in the tumbler. Simon drained the glass and poured himself a second before walking back out to the living room with the glass in one hand and a half-full bottle in the other.

He sat on his couch in the lamplight, sipped his cold whiskey, and listened to a warped Skip James record playing through the rusted horn of an old Victrola he'd found in an alleyway three months earlier, brought upstairs, and repaired. He drank two more glasses of whiskey while the record played. Then it ended and he drank the rest of the whiskey in silence.

*

In his bedroom he undressed down to underwear and T-shirt. He slipped back into his green pajama bottoms and crawled beneath his brown blanket. It felt good to be in bed. He set the alarm clock and dry-swallowed a pill and removed his glasses and set them on the floor. He touched the sore behind his ear and felt the sting of his finger. He stared at the ceiling, his arms at his sides. The ceiling was lined with cracks from various San Andreas renovations. From here on the second floor, with the bedroom window closed, the sounds coming in from Wilshire were muffled, and if you didn't listen closely they combined to create a low electric hum, like a refrigerator. But Simon did listen. He listened to people talking as they walked by on the graffiti-covered sidewalk below. The sound of their voices was comforting. The sound of people reminded him that even if he was set apart somehow, the rest of the world was still close by. It was strange: he didn't usually like to be around people, but he liked to know they were there.

'—just floating around like radio waves and—'

'—what I don't understand is—'

'—and they train you to think it's normal. It's brain-washing and that's—'

Simon closed his eyes. He could hear his heart beating in his chest. He'd been born with a heart murmur. The aortic valve didn't close all the way after blood had been pumped through it, and so some flowed back in, creating an audible murmur and threatening to fuck up the whole works. When Simon was a teenager his human heart valve had been replaced by an artificial heart valve, what they called a caged-ball heart valve. He took blood thinners daily; it was blood thinners in the orange bottle that sat on the floor beside his bed. There was a scar running down the middle of his chest – thick as rope, and meaty as cartilage.

Slowly, the sound of his heartbeat transformed into the sound of a drum, and Simon found himself standing on the sidewalk at a parade as a band stomped by, led by a man with a huge bass drum strapped to his chest: thump-thump, thump-thump. He looked around at the other spectators and found that at the top of their necks were cone-shaped funnels leading to, he somehow knew, other universes, and the funnels were all turned toward him, looking at him, swirling emptiness threatening to suck him in. Their bodies were normal. They wore suits and ties and shorts and dresses, but at the top of each, a swirling vacuum. They walked toward him. Simon turned away from the parade and looked for somewhere to run, but—

A concussion reverberated through the apartment, pulling him out of the beginnings of his dream, and he opened his eyes and saw the ceiling and heard the sound of wood splinters scattering across the living-room floor like shrapnel.

Then silence.

He sat up – the blanket falling off him – and listened.

His head felt swimmy with whiskey, the world Vaseline-lensed, smeared at the edges.

'I know you're here,' a voice said. 'I watched you come in.'

Simon heard footsteps, a *thunk* as something dropped to the floor – in the living room? kitchen? – and then nothing.

He reached out and swept his hand across the grimy floorboards, back and forth, until his fingers brushed across his glasses. He picked them up and put them on, unconsciously hissing at the pain behind his ear – without even realizing he was feeling it – and then got to his feet and padded as quietly as possible to the light switch on the wall. He tried it and got nothing but a *click*.

Did the intruder know where the fuse box was? Had he—

He walked to the dresser. He thought he had a flashlight there, sitting amongst a litter of other things for which there was no specific home. He patted at the surface of the darkness, trying to find the flashlight without knocking anything over, without making any noise at all. He could feel the sweat on his forehead and the once-calming sound of his thumping heartbeat had turned into the pounding of a feral beast trying to escape a cage. Every sound he made was monstrously loud to his own ears. He was sure the intruder could hear everything – could hear the beating of his heart and the labored sound of his breathing and his hands brushing across the various not-flashlights on the top of his dresser.

Finally, his fingers touched a smooth plastic surface –

what he wanted. He picked it up, thumbed a black plastic button, and the flashlight shot out a bright beam of light. Panicked – fuck, he'll see it – he immediately shut it off again.

Then, a moment later, he clicked it back on.

He turned around to face the room and dragged the beam back and forth across the darkness, revealing shifting circles of bedroom – empty corner, closet, blank white wall, mattress covered in rumpled blanket, cracked doorway opening onto the narrow apartment hallway which led to the bathroom in one direction and the living room in the other.

On the other side of the bedroom door, dark silence.

He half expected that when he opened it he would find a vast emptiness littered with pinprick stars and gray planets floating like ghosts in a fog of toxic clouds.

He swallowed.

Why wasn't the intruder making any noise? What was he doing out there?

Simon walked to the bedroom door and pulled it open with trepidation. The hinges squeaked. On the other side was only the hallway – not empty space or pinprick stars or ghost planets – just a narrow strip of floor which led from one room to another.

He stepped into the hallway and went right, to the bathroom, where the apartment ended in a brick wall. He would search the place methodically, starting there.

He tried the switch by the door and again got nothing.

He nodded to himself in the dark – the intruder *had* gotten to the fuse box. There was some small light coming in through the window, however.

The window looked out on the wall of another apartment building. Below it stood a rusty fire escape on which a dead potted ficus, looking like Charlie Brown's Christmas tree, had been sitting since he first moved in, left by the last tenant, or perhaps the tenant before that. In the spring, when Simon moved into the Filboyd Apartments, a mourning dove had laid eggs in the pot, and Simon had watched as the eggs hatched and the chicks left the nest. Strange how, even in a city of millions, all concrete and glass and inhuman machinery, there were little corners where the natural order of things continued.

The apartment directly across from his still had its lights on, and behind the closed white roller shade Simon could see a silhouette of human movement. The silhouette was male. It was doing something that required a lot of arm waving. Simon turned away from the window. He dragged the flashlight beam across his bathroom walls, looked in the corners, looked into the bathtub, and found the room was empty but for him.

He stepped out of the bathroom, closing the door gently behind him. He swallowed and made his way down the hallway toward the living room, checking to make sure his bedroom was still empty before continuing past it. Every step across the creaky floorboards marked his location for the intruder while he himself heard nothing from the other man in his apartment.

He thought he might be walking into a trap, but the alternative was to cower in his bedroom and wait for the intruder to come to him, and that was no alternative at all.

At the end of the hallway he waved the flashlight left and right across the living-room walls, into the corners, seeing no one and nothing. The front door was open and the forty-watt light from the corridor was pouring into the room, lighting up the couch and the end table and Francine the goldfish in her Mason jar, that quart-sized enclosure that made up her entire world.

He walked to the front door and looked out into the corridor, left then right – no one's here, it's safe – and then pushed the door closed. It failed to latch. It simply swung back open about half a foot, allowing the light from the corridor back in. What little of it could squeeze through a six-inch gap, anyway.

He thought whoever broke into his apartment must have looked around, realized he'd broken into the wrong place – oh, hell – and left. He turned away from the door. He could put a chair against it to keep it closed for the remainder of the night. He'd call Leonard tomorrow and tell him what had happened. There was no profit in calling the police if the man had gone; nothing had been stolen so far as he could tell. Aside from his record collection, he didn't think he had anything *worth* stealing.

But then a black shadow lurched from the darkness of the kitchen and put its hands around Simon's throat, and those hands didn't feel like shadows at all. They felt like flesh and bone; they felt like murder.

'Die, you son of a bitch.'

The hands were strong and tight and Simon found it impossible to pull air into his lungs past them. The shadow slammed Simon's back against the door and his head banged against it and dizziness swam over him. The shadow slammed him against the door a second time and he dropped the flashlight. It fell to the floor and a foot kicked it in the scuffle. He grabbed at the hands wrapped around his throat and tried to pry them away, but it proved impossible. The man would not let go. Simon was going to die – as requested.

He swung out blindly at the shadow in front of him and felt his hand weakly punch the side of a head – an ear, a jaw – and the punch, he was sure, did next to no damage, but he knew where the head was now. He swung again, this time with much more force – in a powerful hook aimed for where he thought the face was – and felt his fist slam into a nose, push it sideways, and then something in the nose snapped, and the shadow grunted and its grip loosened. Simon swung again, landing another punch.

He breathed in and his throat stung with the pain of it, but it felt good too. He remembered swimming at a public pool when he was a boy and touching the bottom of a thirteen-foot deep end, and staying down as long as possible, till his vision went gray and his head felt like it might be crushed by the pressure of it all – his ears hurt so much – and how when he surfaced and inhaled that first hot summer lungful it felt like he was breathing for the first time. This felt like that – painful and good and clean and new as a flower that hadn't yet opened.

But then shadow fingers were gripping for his throat yet again, and he was fighting with a man who wanted him dead, and legs got tangled, and he fell to the floor on top of his attacker. He grabbed the man by his neck with his left hand and squeezed it tightly. With his right hand he grabbed the flashlight from the floor and aimed it at the shadow face, making it human.

'Who are you and—'

But then he stopped – was stunned into silence. He knew this man: he had seen him in mirrors, reflected back by rippling lake water, as a ghost in shop windows as he walked by. Simon's hair was gray – almost white – while this man's was a healthy brown; Simon's skin was as pale as the moon while this man had a tan; Simon had no scars on his face, save the acne craters of youth, while this man had a twisted rope of white scar carved into his right cheek; Simon wore glasses while there was nothing between this man's pale green eyes and what he was looking at – but otherwise Simon could have been staring at his twin.

'Jesus,' he said.

And then the man's hand jutted up, quick as a jack-in-the-box, and the fingers clenched Simon's already bruised neck for the third time.

'Die, goddamn you,' the man said. Simon saw the corners of his mouth were crusted with dry spittle and his bloodshot eyes were veined with madness.

Simon did the only thing he could think to do. He slammed the flashlight against the man's head. Blood splattered across Simon's chest and face, staining his T-shirt and dotting the lenses of his glasses, but the hand on his throat did not loosen its grip. If anything, it gripped tighter, with more determination. Simon swung again. The room filled with the scent of copper and sweat, heavy and thick as honey. Enough to make you gag. The grip on his throat loosened, but still he swung – again and again and again. His shoulder ached. His wrist hurt. At some point the cap was knocked off the end of the flashlight and the batteries flew out and scattered across the wood floor and everything went dark, but still he swung. And then he stopped. Finally it was over.

He sat there for a long time, straddling this stranger's chest.

He breathed in and he breathed out.

There'd been moments in his everyday life when he had wondered what it would be like to kill a man. He thought everybody probably had those moments. Those moments made up what he thought of as a person's low life – the internal life they lived but told no one about. Those moments that passed through one's thoughts but didn't so much as ripple the surface of reality. Those moments when an exhausted mother on the verge of losing control thought she just couldn't take the crying any more and considered holding the baby's head underwater. Those moments when a scorned lover thought that if he couldn't have his love, then no one would be allowed to. Those moments when a man looked out of the window, saw a ten-storey drop, and wondered what it would be like to take that final step. But then a pacifier-placated child went quiet, the turmoil of a scorned lover faded, and a man turned away from the window and went back to what he was doing before glancing at that long drop. Of course, sometimes a person's low life broke through the surface, like a breaching whale with an unstoppable momentum. But most of the time killing seemed impossible; most of the time the thought was downright nauseating. There'd been moments in his everyday life when he had wondered what it would be like to kill a man – but until tonight it hadn't happened.

Blood dripped from the flashlight in his hand.

He swallowed back the urge to vomit.

He let go of his grip on the flashlight and it dropped to the floor and rolled in a lazy half circle before coming to a stop. He got to his feet. He took off his glasses and cleaned the blood from them with his T-shirt – the front of which was littered with tiny holes which had been put there by the caps of beer bottles, as he used the shirt to twist the things off – and then put them back onto the bridge of his nose. He walked to the wall and flipped the switch. An empty click. A strange laugh croaked from his throat, and then he felt his way to the kitchen. Then through the kitchen to the fuse box embedded in the back wall, its gray metal door hanging open. He flipped all the switches and various lights throughout the apartment came on, including the lamp on the end table in the living room. The fridge began humming. Someone on the TV chattered about a political controversy.

Simon walked to the living room and shut it off, killing the news mid-sentence.

He looked toward the telephone.

It sat on the floor, a thin gray cord twisting off it, and curling behind the back of the couch. The man who broke into his apartment was stretched out on his back in the middle of the hardwood floor, blood pooling beneath his head. He was wearing an expensive gray suit and a black overcoat. His shoes looked new, except that the toes were scuffed. They were dull-polished, hiding their newness, but Simon saw there was little wear on the heels and only shallow creases in the leather. A green scarf was wrapped around the dead neck, and beneath that and the collar a green tie knotted with a full Windsor. Simon took a few steps toward either the phone or the corpse. He wasn't sure which. He could smell the sweat on the man's skin and the anti-perspirant he'd applied and the stench of beer and an unidentifiable but thick odor beneath that. Perhaps the stink of insanity. Less than a minute ago this man had wanted Simon dead.

'Why?'

His voice sounded strange to his own ears.

The telephone sat on the floor. Simon could see the man's brown wallet poking from the inside pocket of his overcoat.

'Why?'

He glanced toward the telephone once more, and then reached down and slid the wallet from the man's pocket. It was warm from body heat and the leather was smooth in his hand. He flipped it open and looked at the driver's license inside. The dead man's name had been Jeremy Shackleford. He'd lived in Pasadena. Inside the wallet were six crisp hundred-dollar bills, several credit cards, a Ralphs club card, a Borders Rewards card, and an Arclight Cinemas membership card.

Simon tossed the wallet onto the coffee table, and then looked back at Jeremy Shackleford.

'Why did you come here?'

The corpse didn't answer. But then it didn't need to. He had come here to kill Simon. That much was clear. That much was obvious. Why he had wanted Simon dead was the unknown.

A thorough search of Shackleford's person turned up a wad of keys but nothing more; his pockets were otherwise empty, the lint which lined their creases excepted.

Simon put the keys beside the wallet on the coffee table.

'Why?' he said again.

He put a plastic grocery bag over the corpse's head, then wrapped duct tape around the neck, one two three times, taping the bag in place. He tore the tape with his teeth and set the roll aside. If blood continued to ooze from the head it would be contained. Also, Simon did not want to have to look at the corpse's face and see that mouth hanging open, as if on the verge of speaking. *What exactly do you think you're doing, Simon? Don't you think you should be calling the police?* He did not want to have to see those closed eyelids which looked like they might open at any moment. *I can see you, Simon. I know what you did – and I won't forget. I saw it all and I will tell everybody.*

He dragged the body out of the way and laid paper towels over the pool of blood where the head once was. He stood silently and watched the paper towels fade to red. Once he got most of the blood soaked up and the bloody paper towels into a black trash bag, he got on hands and knees with spray cleanser and a scouring sponge and scrubbed away at the red-stained floor. Because the polyurethane finish had been worn off by years of use, blood had gotten into the grain of the wood and Simon couldn't get it all out, but he scrubbed what he could for several minutes, putting all of his weight into it. Once he'd gotten the floor as clean as it was going to get, he threw the sponge into the trash bag with the paper towels. Then he removed his blood-stained T-shirt and threw that into the bag as well. He tied the top of it closed.

He used a coffee mug to bang a nail into the wall outside his apartment and to the left of his front door. Then he tied one end of a shoelace to the doorknob and the other end to the nail. He'd found the shoelace in a drawer in the kitchen, but had no idea where it had come from. Once it was tied in place he nodded. That, he thought, would keep the door from swinging open when he was out. When he was in, he could prop a chair in front of the door to hold it closed. Tomorrow he would buy a padlock to keep the door shut. He didn't want Leonard or any of the handy-men he hired to come into the apartment, which meant he'd have to fix the door himself.

He looked around to see if he'd drawn anyone's attention with his late-night noise-making, but the corridor was empty save for him.

He grabbed the trash bag and headed for the stairs.

He parked his car in front of a 7-Eleven, the fluorescent light from inside spilling out through the dirty windows, splashing across the sun-faded asphalt of the parking lot. He stepped out of the car, carrying the trash bag, and with it he walked around to the back of the convenience store where a dumpster sat smelling of rot. He threw the bag into it.

He stood squinting just inside the door for almost a full minute before his eyes adjusted to the bright lights of the convenience store and he could make out the rows of chips and pork rinds and candy bars and magazines, all foiled in bright blue and green and yellow packaging.

Once his eyes adjusted he made his way to the back of the store, where a white freezer with steel doors sat, a picture of a polar bear holding up a bag of ice on its front. He opened one of the two steel doors and looked inside. He counted eighteen seven-pound bags of ice. He thought his bathtub held sixty gallons, which meant there were about a third as many bags as he needed – give or take. The bags were shy of a gallon, and he wasn't sure exactly how the cubes would pack. About a third of what he needed, minus however many gallons a body took up.

If you rounded down and said a gallon weighed about eight pounds – a gallon of water actually weighed eight-point-three-five pounds – and if you assumed a person weighed about the same – eight pounds per gallon of meat – then Shackleford, if he weighed a hundred and eighty pounds, and that seemed about right to Simon, would take up another twenty-two and a half gallons of space himself.

So to fill the tub Simon needed another twenty or so bags of ice in addition to what was in this freezer.

'Is this all the ice you got?' he asked the man behind the counter.

'You think I'm holding out on you?'

'I don't know.'

'Well, that's where we keep the ice.'

'It's where you keep all the ice?'

'We tried to store extra on the roof, but it kept turning into water.'

After paying for the eighteen bags of ice, Simon loaded the back seat of his car up and headed to another 7-Eleven. There he got another fourteen bags of ice. And at a liquor store near his apartment he got another six bags just to be sure he had enough. Also a bottle of whiskey, since he was out. Then he headed back home.

There was a hole in the grocery bag that he hadn't seen, and as he was carrying the body to the bathroom – struggling: a hundred and eighty pounds was a lot of weight, and this happened to be a hundred and eighty pounds of dead weight – the head rolled right, as if the corpse wanted to see where they were going – watch out you don't bang my head on the wall, buddy – and the blood which had pooled inside drizzled out and onto the hallway floor.

Simon put the body into the tub and cleaned up the

trail of blood. He put the bloody paper towels into his trash can. He thought he should probably get rid of them as he had the others – by dropping them off in some random city dumpster – but it was late, he was tired, and the chances of anyone finding anything were slim. Still, just to be safe, he made sure there was nothing in the trash can with his name on it, a bill or a letter addressed to him. It was clean.

That done, he made several trips up and down the stairs, carrying as much ice as he could in each trip, his arms getting damp and cold, and then numb. He broke open the bags once he got them upstairs, and poured them over the body.

By the time he was done, the ice formed a mound at the top of the tub – like the black dirt on a fresh grave – and only the corpse's head was visible above it. Or rather, the bloody bag which was taped over the corpse's head.

He gathered up the empty plastic bags the ice had come in and threw them on top of the bloody paper towels in his trash can.

He changed back into pajamas, poured himself a whiskey, propped a chair in front of his front door to keep it closed for the night, and walked to the bathroom. He sat on the edge of the tub and sipped his drink.

The ice shifted and settled as it melted. Simon jumped at the sound, then laughed at himself for being so skittish. He took another sip of whiskey.

He felt cold inside. He had killed a man, a man who

was now lying in his bathtub, and he felt almost nothing. He did not feel a loss. He wondered idly if Shackleford's mother was still alive, and if she was whether she'd notice his absence – would phone calls go unanswered? He wondered if Shackleford'd had a wife – and if they'd been on good terms. He reached into the ice and grabbed the left hand and pulled it up to look at it. There was a gold band on the third finger. He wondered if Shackleford and his wife had any children. Would Shackleford's wife look into her son's green eyes and see her missing husband? Did they sit up in bed at night reading novels by Mickey Spillane or biographies of Audrey Hepburn, their feet touching beneath the blankets and sheets, sharing choice bits of text with one another? He wondered how long they had been married. He wondered if Shackleford ever had cause to remove his wedding band. He wondered what his wife tasted like when they kissed. Was her breath sweet? Did her lipstick taste waxy? He wondered what it felt like to have a wife, what it felt like to lie next to someone every night, to feel that warmth.

But mostly he wondered why this man had broken into his apartment, why this man had wanted him dead. For that was why he had come here. This hadn't been a burglary. This had been an attempted murder – a premeditated murder: this man lying dead in Simon's tub had driven here, parked his car, walked up the steps, and broken in through Simon's front door with it in his mind to kill a man.

Why?

Simon couldn't understand it. He lived a quiet life. He had never hurt a soul – until now, and this was self-defense. He couldn't imagine why anyone would want him dead. How anyone could be filled with so much rage, and all of it directed at him.

He sipped his whiskey and felt cold inside.

The ice shifted again. A sound came from the grocery bag. Simon reached over and put his drink on the small bathroom counter. He leaned closer to the grocery bag and thought he sensed movement – very slight movement – perhaps caused by shallow breathing. Was Shackleford still alive – unconscious but breathing low? The thought made Simon's stomach feel sour.

Would he be able to dash out this man's brains while he lay unconscious in his tub? Would he be able to simply dash out this man's brains in cold blood, for no other purpose than to have it done? And if he couldn't, what was he going to do with him? Let him go?

Simon leaned closer, hoping he was mistaken – maybe it was just the sound of the ice shifting again – but he wasn't. He wasn't mistaken.

Shackleford's cold left hand shot up and grabbed a handful of Simon's gray hair and yanked it hard, slamming Simon's head against the blue art deco tiles that lined the wall around the tub. The pain was immediate and a star burst exploded in front of his eyes. He slipped off the edge of the tub and thudded to the floor with a clacking of teeth. He heard the ice shifting, felt cubes of it falling out of the tub around him and on him, and then something heavy – something which weighed about a hundred and eighty pounds – was on top of him. It was cold as a corpse, wet, and slippery as a fish.

Simon blinked away the blindness and saw floating above him a white plastic grocery bag. There was a hole in the front of it and it dripped blood onto his face, into his mouth – salty and thick and metallic – and through the hole he could see one pale green eye staring at him, bright and alive and filled with rage and insanity.

He reached behind him for a weapon of some kind – I'm not going to die on the floor in my own bathroom for no reason at all – and knocked over a magazine rack, sending the glossy things sliding across the tiles. The next thing to fall was a toilet plunger, and then a toilet brush. Water spilled out of the cup the brush had been sitting in, stale and reeking.

Simon's vision was fading and going smeary at the edges and the colors were distorting, becoming bright and strange, everything turning blue and green and grainy as an old film.

And then he felt it.

A porcelain jar out of which a small bamboo plant was growing. It was the only plant in Simon's apartment, and he took great care to make sure it stayed alive. Filled with water and small stones, the porcelain jar was heavy.

Simon wrapped his hand around it and swung his

arm forward like a catapult, smashing the thing into his attacker's face. A moment later blood came gushing from the hole in the bag and the bag sagged with the weight of what blood could not escape it. Simon wrapped his hands around Shackleford's throat and squeezed as hard as he could, gritting his teeth, feeling the veins in his temples pulsing, feelings the cords in his neck go taut. His heart was pounding in his chest.

Shackleford went limp, but Simon wasn't going to fall for it this time. He let the body drop to the cold tile floor and then crawled atop it and continued to throttle the neck. And then he picked up the porcelain jar again – now slick and smeared with blood – and slammed it against Shackleford's head. It was an easy thing to do when there was no face to look at. He might have been cracking a walnut. He slammed the jar against the head a dozen times, breathing hard. With each hit, what was behind the bag went softer and softer as the bone of the skull broke into smaller and smaller pieces. The porcelain jar finished what the plastic flashlight had begun.

He got to his feet, feeling weak and lightheaded, swaying on his legs like a top-heavy tree in a strong wind. He swung a leg and landed a kick into Shackleford's ribs, but when he kicked again he lost his footing and fell to the floor, sitting in the stinking water that was running along the grout lines.

He sat there, sprawled out, legs in front of him, hands pressed against the tile behind him, holding him up, and stared a blank moment. His chest hurt from heavy breathing. His throat was sore and bruised and it hurt to pull air through it.

'Jesus,' he said, and then looked at Shackleford. 'You better stay dead this time.'

He crawled toward the bathroom counter, grabbed his whiskey, and downed it in a single draught. It burned going down.

He sat down on the couch with the telephone in his lap. He dialed Dr Zurasky. He hadn't talked to Zurasky in over a year – since last April or May – but for some reason he was the first person Simon thought to call. He didn't know why. He couldn't tell him what had happened. He just wanted someone to talk to. After four rings that someone picked up and said, ''Lo?'

'Dr Zurasky, it's Simon Johnson.'

'Who?'

'Simon Johnson.'

'I don't – never mind that. It's late.'

'I know. I'm sorry. It's just—'

'Is it an emergency?'

'I don't—'

'This is my emergency line. It says so right on my card. Is this an emergency?'

'No, I guess not.'

'Are you thinking of harming yourself?'

'No.'

'Are you thinking of harming someone else?'

Simon paused. Then: 'No.'

'Okay,' Dr Zurasky said. 'Call my office tomorrow morning at nine. Tell my assistant Ashley I said to squeeze you into the schedule. What was your name again?'

'Simon Johnson.'

'Right.'

The click of a signal being severed.

'Oh,' Simon said. 'Okay.'

He put the phone back into its cradle and set it on the floor. For a moment he thought about calling Robert or Chris, but then decided against it. No good would come of it. He got to his feet and padded to his bedroom.

He awoke with a bit of a hangover. His throat hurt. He stumbled to the bathroom, wetted a washcloth, wiped himself down with it – the bathtub being in use – brushed his teeth, and combed his hair. There were two dark blue-green thumbprint bruises on the front of his neck, and eight barely noticeable fingerprint bruises stitching their way up the back, right into his hairline. He was surprised the bruises weren't worse. He looked at the corpse in the bathtub. A lot of the ice had melted in the night and gone clear – before, it had been frosty white – and he could now see the body beneath. It was strange, like an insect in amber.

He walked out of the bathroom, down the hall, and into the kitchen.

There was a screwdriver on the kitchen floor, partly hidden beneath the edge of the counter. It was a Phillips head with a black and yellow plastic handle. According to the same handle it was a Stanley screwdriver.

He picked it up and put it into a junk drawer.

He packed his lunch.

He grabbed Shackleford's wallet and keys and headed out through the front door.

He pushed his way out of the Filboyd Apartments and walked along Wilshire toward his car. As he walked he kicked a pack of Camel Filters – his brand – picked up the box, shook it, found it was empty, and dropped it again. Then he saw the dog just to his left. It was in the gutter, its head resting on the curb, which was smeared with blood. He recognized its chewed-on steak-fat ear. It lay dead behind a black Saab sedan. Its mouth was open, its tongue hanging out. The car was no more than two years old and had blood streaked across its otherwise white rear license plate.

Poor bastard.

Simon briefly considered keying the Saab, scratching something awful into the door, but decided against it.

He continued on to his Volvo.

*

He sat at his desk and dialed the number.

Ashley picked up on the other end. 'Dr Zurasky's office.'

'Hello. This is Simon Johnson. Dr Zurasky was expecting me to make an appointment for today, and—'

'He said you'd be calling. Have you seen Dr Zurasky before? He wasn't—'

'I'm actually feeling much better today, so I'm just gonna hold off.'

A pause, and then: 'Okay. I'll let him know.'

'Thank you.'

He hung up the telephone.

Then he saw something out of the corner of his eye. He glanced left and there was his boss, Bernard Thames, a pear-shaped man in his fifties with narrow shoulders and a wide middle. Big forehead a beach over which the wave of his bangs splashed, eyebrows like question marks, long and narrow fingers with knuckles like knots, fingernails trimmed so short a couple of them were bloody. He wore gray suits and spoke in an inflectionless monotone. But Simon thought there might have been more to him than was immediately obvious – Mr Thames often wore red socks.

He had no idea how long his boss had been standing there.

'Yes, sir?'

'About the Samonek account.'

'If you mean the discrepancy between the check and

the time card for Fran Lewis, it's the time card that's in error. I got a last-minute phone call from Sheryl on Wednesday. I must have forgotten to update and initial the time card.'

Mr Thames nodded a quick affirmation, tipping his chin briefly.

'Okay,' he said. 'That answers that.'

He turned to walk away, managed three steps, and then turned back.

'I've been meaning to ask you,' he said, 'did you call the office a couple nights ago?'

'No, sir.'

'Are you sure?'

'Yes, sir. I don't recall ever having called the office after business hours.'

'That's what I thought. Strange.'

'Someone called?'

'Someone claiming to be you called and left a message. Apologized for missing so much work, and then asked for his job back. It didn't make sense.'

'No, sir. I haven't missed a day yet.'

'I know. I checked your file.'

'Oh.'

'You have no idea what it might be about?'

'Not the foggiest.'

Mr Thames nodded and frowned, as if that was what he had expected to hear but had been hoping for more. Then he simply stood and stared for a moment.

'Is that all?' Simon asked.

Mr Thames blinked and looked around like he didn't know how he'd gotten there, smiled a smile that could have meant anything, and said, 'Yes, indeed.'

'Okay, sir.'

Mr Thames turned and walked away, each step he took momentarily revealing a thin slice of red sock before the gray pants fell down to cover it again.

When Simon stepped out of the office building and into the noontime sun, Robert and Chris were nowhere to be seen. He figured they'd gotten tired of waiting for him – it had taken longer than usual for the twentieth floor to clear out – and headed to Wally's without him. They had been doing that more and more frequently.

He lighted a cigarette and started his walk toward Broadway.

When he arrived at the diner, he found both of his friends at a booth against the back wall. They were sitting next to one another.

The diner walls were thin wood paneling and the tables which littered the room were white with specks of blue and scratched and stained as well. The chairs were a mishmash, some metal, some wood, some plastic, no two alike. The diner had a 'B' rating – maybe cockroaches had been found in the kitchen, or the refrigeration system wasn't quite up to code – and in a fit of humor someone had spray-painted a graffito on the glass window in which the 'B' was posted to make it the beginning of a claim of quality.

 E∫T FOOD IN TOWN!

it said. Simon could neither confirm nor deny the claim, since he'd never ordered a meal here.

He walked across the scarred vinyl floor to the booth where Robert and Chris were sitting.

'Hey, Simon,' Chris said.

'Hey.'

'How you doing?' Robert said.

Simon sat down across from them, shrugged.

'I'm good. Did you guys order already?'

'Yeah, it's on the way,' Chris said. 'Did you watch that UFO special last night?'

'What UFO special?'

'The one about UFOs.'

'No,' Simon said. 'I had company. Was it any good?'

'Was it any good? Are you fucking *kidding* me? It was about UFOs. Of *course* it was good. Those fuckers'll get you, man. I told you to watch it. I can't believe you forgot.'

'You never mentioned it.'

'When we talked on the phone the other night. Man, you got a memory like a cheesecloth.'

'When we talked on the phone the other night?'

'When you called me.'

'I didn't call you.'

''Course you called me.'

'You had company?' Robert said.

'Well – not company exactly. Someone broke into my apartment.'

'God*damn*, man,' Chris said. 'I told you you should move outta that dump and into a proper apartment. Were you home?'

'Yeah,' Simon said. 'I was in bed.'

'Are those bruises on your neck?' Robert said. 'What happened?'

'He broke in through the front door.'

'After that.'

Simon opened his mouth but nothing came out.

Babette arrived carrying a brown tray and gnawing on her gum like a horse on cud. She put chipped white plates with sandwiches and fries in front of Robert and Chris, and then put Simon's 7-Up on the table in front of him.

'Hi, Simon,' she said, smiling.

Babette was almost pretty. She was in her mid-thirties, and her face was a smooth oval framed by boyishly short brunette hair. Her lips were thick and red and looked very soft. She had a large backside and a narrow waist, where her body bent forward like an elbow, maybe from the weight of her breasts, which were sizable. Somehow, she reminded Simon of a rather sexy ostrich.

'Hi, Babette,' he said, smiling back. 'I like your lipstick.'

'Aw, you're too sweet. *Thank* you.'

'Sure.'

Then she pivoted on a dirty white sneaker and bounced away like a beach ball.

Simon took the paper off the top of his straw and drew in a swallow of 7-Up. There was something black floating on the surface of the liquid. Simon thought it was a piece of ground pepper. He dipped a finger in, got whatever it was on the tip of it, and then wiped it off on his pants. If he didn't like Babette he might complain. But he did like her.

He unpacked his lunch, laid it out in front of him, and began to work on a sandwich.

Chris smiled at him. 'I think Babette's sweet on you.'

'No,' Simon said. 'She's just working for tips.'

'But what happened with the break-in?' Robert said.

Simon licked his lips, swallowed, looked toward the wall where ketchup was splattered, a dried chunk of it hanging between two wood panels like a bloody booger.

'I'd rather not talk about it.'

'There was this one guy,' Chris said, 'UFO took him for a month, but it only felt like a couple of hours to him, though, right? So he gets home and he's lost his job and his wife is banging some neighbor and his dog ran off. Sounds like a country song, huh? Except for the UFO bit. But it's true. It happens more than you think. Aliens are all around us, and the only way you can identify 'em is by their eyes. They got crazy eyes. They look like—'

'Would you shut up?' Robert said.

'Why?'

'I don't want to hear about UFOs.'

'But they're interesting.'

'Not to me, they aren't.'

'Well, that's 'cause you only like boring shit. Probably wanna talk about Dustonsky or some other German writer.'

'Dostoevsky. And he was Russian.'

'Whatever, man. He's still dead.'

Simon got to his feet after only a few bites of sandwich. He decided he wasn't feeling hungry.

'Where you going?' Robert said.

'I don't feel so hot.'

'You sick?'

Simon shook his head.

'No, I'm just—'

He let it end there, then walked toward the front door. As he did, Babette smiled at him from where she was standing at the counter. 'Bye, Simon,' she said. 'See you tomorrow.'

'See you tomorrow, Babette.'

He grabbed the door handle.

'Oh, wait,' Babette said.

'What is it?'

'Do you—' Babette began, and then took her gum from her mouth, apparently thinking this conversation was too serious for chewing. 'Do you have a brother?'

Simon shrugged. 'I don't think so. Why?'

'Some guy came in here yesterday asking about you and acting really strange.'

'What'd he look like?'

'You. Kinda. That's why I asked if you had a brother.'

'Yeah – no. I don't think so. I was adopted.'

'I didn't know that.'

'Yeah.'

'So you don't know anything about—'

Simon shook his head. 'Nope.'

'Okay,' she said. She bit her lip and seemed unsure about what to say next. Finally: 'See you tomorrow.'

'See you tomorrow, Babette.'

'Okay.'

'Okay.'

She put the gum back into her mouth – peeling it off the tip of her finger with her teeth – and turned around to get back to work.

For the rest of his lunch break Simon sat in his cubicle flipping through a newspaper, glancing at headlines to see if anything struck him as worth reading. But it wasn't a headline that caught his eye; it was a photograph. The picture was of an old man with parentheses stacked up on either side of his mouth, with loose skin hanging below his chin despite the fact that he was thin, with bags under his eyes that could hold a pint apiece. The headline read

GERMAN DIRECTOR HELMUT MÜLLER KILLED

and the piece continued

LOS ANGELES – Controversial German film-maker Helmut Müller, who wrote and directed Nazi propaganda films such as *U-Boote westwärts* and *Kolberg* before immigrating to the United States and making such anti-war classics as *The Last Coffin* and *Gunmen Die Too*, was found dead outside his Koreatown apartment early yesterday evening, the apparent victim of a mugging. He was ninety-seven years old.

Müller, who hadn't directed a film since the 1966 box-office and critical failure *Hell's Mouth*, had condemned film as being 'inherently incapable of purity or honesty'. He asserted that the 'dream of an artist is always pure', in an essay for the now-defunct *Los Angeles Free Press*, 'but we contaminate it with our mental illnesses in the act of creation. I do not agree with Freud. I do not believe dreams are evidence of anything; only how we corrupt our dreams when trying to realize them is evidence. The difficulty lies in telling where the dream ends and the corruption begins. Dreams come to us fully formed, as gifts from the gods, and we destroy them. It is best to leave them in the ether where they can remain holy.' He gave up film-making for good in 1970, after over twenty-seven years and twenty-two films, opting instead to open a restaurant in Sherman Oaks. 'Feeding people,' he said at the time, 'is at least honest work.' The restaurant closed in 1982, and Müller had since been in retirement.

The Academy of Motion Picture Arts and Sciences had planned on honoring the film-maker with a lifetime achievement award in 2002, but plans were dropped when his previously buried past as a Nazi propagandist was brought to the public eye by protesters. When asked for his response to the Academy's dropped plans to honor him, he said, 'I would not honor me. What I have done is unforgivable. I have spent the last fifty-seven years trying to redeem myself. But I do not believe that I have, or that I will before I retire from this earth. But it is a relief that it is out. It was a terrible secret to keep.'

In 2005 Mr Müller spoke at the Los Angeles Film Academy about 'the importance of telling truth to power, whatever the consequences', but noted that this advice was 'coming from the lips of a famous coward. I was worse than silent. I let oppressors and murderers speak through me. This is an unforgivable sin – to allow something as holy as art to be used for evil. Unforgivable.' This was his last public speech.

All three of Mr Müller's children are deceased. He is survived by four grandchildren and six great-grandchildren.

Simon read the piece twice, and then folded up the newspaper and dropped it into the trash can under his desk. He looked at the clock. His lunch break was over.

*

The Pasadena street on which Jeremy Shackleford once lived was just off Colorado Boulevard. It was a quiet, tree-lined strip of pothole-free asphalt dotted with late-model cars, old but well-maintained three- and four-bedroom houses, and green yards. The sidewalks were covered in faded chalk hopscotch etchings and jump-rope scars, and were cracked in a few places by tree roots that had gotten bigger than expected; but the gutters were free of trash – no paper cups and condom wrappers here – the driveways were free of oil stains, and the yards were free of weeds. Despite the sound of traffic from Colorado, the street had an air of calm about it.

Simon drove his old rattling Volvo along the asphalt, glancing from the driver's license in his left hand, pinched between thumb and index finger, to the numbers painted curbside. He found parking right out front, pulled to the curb, and killed the engine.

Above him, the orange sun shot daggers through the branches of one of the many eucalyptus trees which lined the street, creating a strange pattern of shadows on the car, a natural stencil painted with light.

He looked to his right and saw the Shackleford house through his water-spotted passenger-side window. It was a Craftsman-style building, set at the top of five concrete steps which had been painted green, and half-hidden behind a plant-littered front porch. Basil and rosemary and aloe grew there, as well as ficus and three hanging pots spilling vines dotted with large purple flowers.

He tossed Shackleford's driver's license onto the passenger's seat beside the wallet from which he'd pulled it and stepped out of his Volvo. He did not lock the doors. In this neighborhood he doubted anyone would even glance in the direction of his battered car, and if they did they would no doubt assume it belonged to someone's maid. Or perhaps someone's child visiting from USC or UCLA, home so mom could do the laundry.

He walked up the concrete path that cut the green yard in two, made his way up the painted steps, and, standing in front of the door, took a deep breath. He felt nervous and afraid. His chest hurt. His body shook slightly. He doubted anyone would notice just by looking at him, but he could feel it.

He thumbed the doorbell and heard the muffled sound of it chiming inside.

There was no response.

He rang again, and again there was no response, no sound of footsteps rushing to reach the door, no request to hold on just a moment, I'll be right there, I'm in the kitchen and my hands are full. There was only silence.

He looked over his left shoulder and saw a man of retirement age walking his dog. Or rather, the dog was walking him, leaning forward and pulling the old man behind it on its leash. The old man was paying Simon no attention. And a moment later he was past, being pulled forward by his eager dog while leaning against the force like a man in a windstorm trying to maintain equilibrium.

Over his right shoulder, Simon saw a pair of blonde girls, wearing identical flower-print dresses and red ribbons in their hair, hunched over something on their lawn, their backs to him. With those exceptions, the neighborhood appeared to be empty.

And still no one opened the front door.

He rang the doorbell a third time just to be sure.

Then – after a moment – pulled Shackleford's wad of keys from his pocket. He tried three or four of them before he found the one that could unlock the front door, and with it he did so. He pushed the door open, stepped just inside, and closed it behind him. He put the keys back into his pocket and twisted the deadbolt home.

The house appeared to be empty of life, but it also seemed to be humming; the electricity in here tingled on his skin and in his hair. The living room had polished hardwood floors. The walls were a warm orange, the ceiling a darker version of the same. A flat-panel television hung on the living-room wall above the fireplace hearth, black plastic surrounding a black screen, a small red light glowing in the lower right-hand corner of the frame. The fireplace itself was simply ornamental now, the one-inch stub of gas pipe sticking from the wall capped off long ago. Several candles sat on the bricks in front of it. A plush brown couch sat atop an area rug that was thick and tightly woven. Expensive-looking art hung on the walls. The living room was the size of Simon's entire apartment.

Shackleford: this was where he'd lived.

Why had he wanted Simon dead?

The orange walls wouldn't tell him, nor the television, nor the floor beneath his feet.

As Simon wandered through the house, he found a picture of Shackleford and a brunette woman, a woman he assumed was Shackleford's wife. She was about six inches shorter than him, which would make her five three, hair shoulder-length, eyes the color of a clear blue sky. Her skin was smooth and white, her lips pink and soft-looking, her neck graceful and thin and long. She was wearing a gray blouse with the top two buttons undone, revealing the shallow cleavage of a small-breasted woman in a push-up bra. She wasn't smiling save in one corner of her mouth, but her eyes were alive with humor. She and Shackleford were arm in arm.

The picture was in a four-by-six-inch frame, and Simon slipped it into the outside pocket of his brown corduroy coat.

The dining room had been converted into an office. There was a desk against one wall with a computer atop it. The computer's screen was black. There were stacks of paperwork on either side of the keyboard. On the wall opposite the desk, three waist-high bookshelves filled with books on mathematics. The books seemed to be organized by difficulty rather than alphabetically. Several of them were textbooks.

Simon walked to the desk and sat down in a black leather chair. He grabbed a stack of paperwork from the desk and set it in his lap and flipped through it. He found gas bills, cable bills, directions to various locations, torn bits of paper with phone numbers scrawled across them, penciled names of authors, and doodles of penises and breasts and eyes, sometimes in odd combination. And at the bottom of the stack he found a folder filled with math tests for an Algebra I class, a class that had apparently been taught at Pasadena College of the Arts, a class that had apparently been taught by Dr Jeremy Shackleford. They were from a summer session, now surely over.

A mathematics instructor. Pasadena College of the Arts.

Simon was setting the stack of paperwork back onto the desk when he heard a key sliding into the front door. He turned to face the sound and heard the lock tumble.

He jumped to his feet and frantically looked for a place to hide.

The doorknob rattled.

There was a coat closet on the other side of the room. He ran for it.

'Jeremy?' the woman said.

Simon recognized her from the photograph. Her voice was smoky but still feminine and very melodic; she almost sounded as if she were singing when she spoke. She stood near the couch, purse still over her shoulder, keys still in hand. Simon could smell her from where he stood: a light, clean sweat and bar soap and lotion and some kind of fruit-scented shampoo.

He could feel hangers poking into his back and the arms of leather and wool coats brushing against his wrists and hands. It gave him the creepy sensation that people were standing behind him. He could smell the closed-off smell all closets seemed to possess, despite the slats in the door. He watched the woman on the other side through those slats, waiting to see if she would somehow sense his presence.

She looked around the living room, and for a moment seemed to look right at him through the door. Simon's breath caught in his throat. He swallowed and it stung. His neck was still swollen.

She pulled her purse off her arm and tossed it onto the back of the couch, and then grabbed a remote from the couch's arm. She clicked on the television – a local news program. Some woman with short blonde hair was talking about the Los Angeles Department of Water and Power dumping plastic balls into the Ivanhoe Reservoir in order to protect it from the sun's rays and keep birds from shitting in it.

What's your name? Simon wondered.

The woman muted the television and looked around. 'Jeremy?'

Had he said it aloud? He didn't think he had. She couldn't have heard him.

Maybe he had.

'You're going crazy, Samantha,' she said to herself. She turned the television's volume back on, watched the news for a moment or two longer, and then set the remote back down on the arm of the couch and walked away. She disappeared into a hallway.

Her name was Samantha.

Simon wondered what it was like to live with her. He wondered what it would be like to look into the eyes of a woman like that and have her tell you she loves you; he wondered what it would be like to tell her you love her, too.

He pushed open the closet door and stepped out into the living room. He closed the closet door behind him.

He walked softly across the hardwood floor and once he'd nearly reached the hallway he stopped. He leaned forward and looked around the corner. At the end of the hallway was an open door, and on the other side was Samantha. She was sitting on a toilet, her skirt bunched up around her waist and panties stretched like a rubber band between her knees. She was reading a magazine with an actress on its glossy cover.

'Samantha,' he said in a low whisper. 'Your name is Samantha.'

He walked to the front door, grabbed the doorknob. He turned it carefully and pulled the door open – pausing momentarily when it squeaked, glancing back over his shoulder, seeing nothing, and continuing – and then he stepped out into the early-evening sunlight.

*

He walked toward the street, looking around, feeling paranoia flowing cold through his veins, throbbing at his
temples like a headache.

Samantha's car was in the driveway now, parked on
the right side, a dark blue Mercedes, perhaps the same year
as Simon's Volvo, but in much better shape, paint new,
well-oiled leather interior uncracked by the sun.

He walked past it, reached the street, slid onto his torn-
up driver's seat, and tried to slam the door shut behind
him, but it banged against the metal seatbelt clip and
bounced open again. He grabbed the clip and pulled the belt
over his chest and waist and latched it, then tried the door
a second time. This time it stayed closed. He started his
car, turned it around, and drove down the street the same
way he had come.

The two blonde girls in the flower-print dresses with
red ribbons in their hair were still in their yard. Simon
glanced at them as he drove, and though he might have
been mistaken, he would've sworn they were taking turns
poking a dead cat with a stick.

He pushed through the smudged glass doors and into
the lobby of the Filboyd Apartments carrying a plastic bag
from the hardware store he'd stopped at on the way home.
He headed up the dark stairwell toward his apartment,
smelling stale urine as he went. At the top of the stairs, he

saw his landlord hadn't yet gotten someone to clean up the graffito painted there.

WELL, TAKE HIM

it still said, somewhat impatiently.

When he turned left at the head of the stairs, he saw Robert standing in the corridor by his front door. His arms were crossed and he was leaning against the wall.

Simon's stomach clenched as if squeezed by a fist. Why was he here?

After a moment: 'Hi.'

'I got a flat tire. Hoping to use your phone.'

'Flat tire?'

'Yeah, over on Normandie.'

'Normandie? Don't you live off Western?'

'You can't choose where to get a flat.'

'You don't have a cell phone?'

Although Simon himself didn't have one, it seemed odd to him; everybody had a cell phone these days.

'I do,' Robert said, pulling it from his pocket and holding it up, 'but I dropped it in the toilet at work when I was pulling up my pants. Fried it.'

'Oh.'

'Is it a problem?'

Simon tried to smile but it felt like a grimace. All he could think of was the corpse in his bathtub.

'Of course not,' he said.

He walked to the front door and unhooked the shoelace from the nail in the wall. The front door swung open on its own. It occurred to him now how dumb it had been to leave his apartment unsecured like that. He should have done something to keep the apartment closed off this morning. Well, what was done was done. There was no point in worrying over—

'Come on in.'

They stepped over the splinters of wood still on the floor.

Simon pushed the door shut behind them, and then shoved the back of a chair under the doorknob to keep it closed.

'Go ahead and call whoever you need to. Want a drink?'

'Sure.'

Simon nodded, then headed into the kitchen.

The two men sat on the couch with their whiskeys. Someone from the auto club would be arriving within thirty minutes. Simon watched Francine pull fish food from the neuston at the water's surface and into her black mouth. He wanted Robert out of his apartment.

He had done Robert a favor a few months ago, a big one – it was how they'd become friends – but it wasn't the kind of favor that would allow Simon to show the man the corpse in his tub. Robert might have been beaten to a pulp and/or spent a few months in a Tijuana jail cell without Simon's help – but months were not years.

He wanted Robert out of his apartment.

Robert took a swallow of his whiskey.

'You never said what happened last night.'

'Yeah,' he said. It was all he could think to say.

'So?'

'It's not even worth discussing, really.'

'What else are we gonna talk about? Politics?' He said this last word with disgust.

Simon exhaled in a sigh, took a sip of his whiskey.

'This guy broke into my apartment. I heard the noise and came out to the living room. I'd been in bed. He was digging through my record collection. I have a lot of old records. Maybe he followed me home from the record shop on La Brea on Saturday. I don't know. Anyways, when he saw me, he attacked. I fought back, but . . . he must have brained me or something.' He shook his head to demonstrate his confusion. 'When I woke up he was gone.'

Robert looked at the record collection.

'It doesn't look like he took anything.'

'He must have panicked after the confrontation.'

'Maybe,' Robert said.

Simon reached into the inside pocket of his corduroy sport coat and pulled out his Camel Filters and his Zippo lighter. He lighted a cigarette. Usually he didn't smoke inside. He hated the stale smell of cigarettes lingering in a room. Usually he climbed through the bathroom window and smoked on his fire escape if he didn't want to trudge all the way downstairs. But he was nervous and he needed to be doing something, and the bathroom was not available. He inhaled deeply.

'You all right?' Robert asked.

Simon glanced at him. Was there a look of suspicion in Robert's eyes? Simon thought perhaps there was. Something about the way his eyebrows were cocked, the way his head was tilted, like a cat about to pounce on a mouse, a twitch at the corner of his mouth.

'Yeah,' Simon said. 'I guess I'm more upset by the break-in than I realized.'

Robert nodded. Then he drained the rest of the whiskey from his glass, set it on the coffee table, and got to his feet. He twisted his neck around, sending out several pops from between the vertebrae.

'I'm gonna take a leak.'

He started for the bathroom.

'No, wait!'

Robert paused at the head of the hallway.

'What?'

'The toilet's broken. It doesn't flush.'

'It's probably just the chain. I'll reach into the tank and pull the stopper manually. If I can fix it, I will.'

Then he continued down the hallway.

Simon got to his feet. He took two steps toward the hallway and then stopped. He didn't know what to do. He couldn't attack his friend. He could, but that might be as bad as him finding the body. No, it wouldn't. He had to stop him from going into the bathroom.

'Robert, no,' he said as he rushed into the hallway. 'It's not the—'

But it was too late.

'What the fuck?' Robert said from the bathroom.

Simon stopped mid-stride. He looked at Robert, who was standing in the open doorway, facing the bathtub.

He pulled a lungful from his cigarette. He swallowed.

'Robert,' he said.

Robert looked at him.

'What the fuck?'

'What?' he said, as he walked into the bathroom.

'There's a fucking dead guy in your bathtub, man.'

'I know – I put him there.'

'*Why?*' Robert said.

'He broke into my apartment.'

'I don't care if he raped your goldfish. You don't store a corpse in your apartment. You have to call the police.'

Simon felt as if someone was slowly drilling a wood screw into his forehead, just above his left eye, and his left eye was leaking water as a result of this. It ran down his cheek and he wiped it away with the back of one hand.

'You have to call the police,' Robert said again.

Simon took off his glasses, pulled his shirts out of his

waistband, used the T-shirt to wipe off the lenses, wiped at his eye again, and replaced the glasses.

'I can't,' he said finally. 'I can't call the police.'

'Why not?'

'Because there's a dead guy in my bathtub, Robert. A dead guy who's been on ice for almost a full day. The police won't just let that go.'

'Well, why the fuck did you put him on ice?'

'I didn't want to call the police. I wanted to buy myself some time.'

'For what?'

Simon closed his eyes, head throbbing. He let out a sigh and tried to ignore what his mind was telling him was the easiest way to solve this problem – which was to kill Robert. Robert was his friend, his only close friend – as close a friend as he'd ever had, anyway – and he couldn't just kill him. He couldn't simply steal forty or fifty years of breath from him because he had become a problem, especially since it was Simon's own fault. He could have found a reason to keep Robert out. And yet a disturbing voice in his head – the voice that narrated his low life – kept insisting that murder was the simple solution: Just kill him, Simon. You've already killed once. It wasn't so bad, was it? You didn't even lose an entire night's sleep. So do it. Do it and get it done with. Sure, it's your fault. You fucked up. So fix your mistake. You pay or Robert does. Kill him. Kill him and be done with it. It'll only take a few minutes and then it'll be over.

Simon opened his eyes.

'What?' he said.

'You needed to buy time for what?'

'He broke into my apartment to kill me,' he said. 'I need to find out why.'

'You said yourself he attacked you because you caught him going through your record collection.'

'Well, I didn't catch him doing anything. He broke in and he tried to murder me and that's all he tried to do. I need to know why. And look.'

Simon reached down and started pulling the duct tape away from the corpse's neck.

'What the fuck are you doing?' Robert said. 'I don't want to see this.'

'Just hold on. Maybe it'll help you understand.'

'I already understand. You killed a man and now—'

Simon pulled the plastic bag away and Robert went silent. Blood dripped from the bag, and Simon thought of times he had purchased a hamburger and the packaging had leaked.

'Jesus,' Robert said. 'You didn't say—' He put his hand over his open mouth. 'I – who is he?'

'Jeremy Shackleford. He taught math at the Pasadena College of the Arts.'

'Why did he break into your place?'

'I told you,' Simon said. 'To kill me. He broke in because he wanted me dead.'

'Why?'

Simon shook his head.

'I don't know.'

He reached down and put the bag back over the corpse's head.

Both men simply stood silent for a long moment.

Finally, Robert said, 'I've – I've seen him before.'

'When?'

'I don't know,' Robert said. 'Monday maybe. Is today Thursday?'

'I don't know. What happened?'

'Remember when I told you a guy accosted me on the street?'

Simon nodded. He remembered. Robert had even mentioned that the guy looked a bit like him. He couldn't believe he hadn't thought of that till now.

'This is him. I was walking to that liquor store on Fourth Street to get a pack of smokes and he grabbed me by the shirt and slammed me against a wall and asked me if I was the one who took it.'

'Took what?'

'I don't know.'

'What did you tell him?'

'I told him I didn't.'

'What are you gonna do now?'

'I don't know,' Simon said. 'Now that you know, I was – I was hoping you could help me figure that out.'

Robert was shaking his head before Simon even got the sentence out.

'No,' he said. 'No way. I don't – I never. No. No.'

Simon and Robert had been sitting on the couch, but now Robert got to his feet.

'I'm gonna wait for the auto club outside.'

'You don't want another drink?'

Robert shook his head.

'Are you sure?'

'Yeah,' Robert said. 'I'm – ' he licked his lips and swallowed – 'yeah, I'm okay. I have to drive. I'm gonna go.'

Simon felt a sudden desperation to keep Robert there. In part because if Robert left Simon didn't know what he would do – maybe he would go straight to the police – but mostly because he simply didn't want to be alone right now. Thinking of the life Shackleford must have lived with his wife and his students and his university friends made Simon feel hollow in his own. What did he have? His record collection and his whiskey. And Francine, of course. But it wasn't enough.

'Are you sure?' he asked.

'Yeah. I'm just gonna wait outside.'

'Please. Just stay for one more drink.'

'I'll see you tomorrow.'

Robert walked to the front door and pulled the chair away from it.

'I'll see you tomorrow,' he said again, and then pulled open the door.

'Robert.'

Robert stopped. He turned and looked at Simon.

'Don't go to the police. Please. I need to find out why he wanted me dead.'

Robert bit his lip, looked out into the corridor – maybe thinking of Tijuana and his trouble there – and then he looked back.

'I didn't see a thing,' he said finally. He swallowed. 'And now we're square.'

Simon stared down at the ice in his glass for a long moment.

'Simon?'

He looked up at Robert.

'If I keep quiet,' he said, 'we're square. I don't owe you anything else.'

Simon nodded.

'Okay.'

Robert stepped out of the front door, pulling it shut behind him, but it only swung back open again. Simon listened to him walk across the corridor floor and then down the stairs to the lobby, shoes clunking against wood. Then he was gone.

Simon poured himself another drink, sipped it.

When he leaned back he felt something large and heavy in his pocket. He reached in and pulled it out. It was the picture of Jeremy Shackleford and Samantha he had taken from their house. He looked at it for a long time, at Samantha's smile, at how beautiful she was. It must have been wonderful to have a woman like that, to be able to call a woman like that your own. Simon imagined sleeping beside her, spooned up against her bottom, one arm wrapped around her, hand cupping a firm breast. He imagined he'd be able to feel her slow heart beating in her chest.

He set the picture down on the coffee table and looked at it for a while longer.

Then he got to his feet, found a screwdriver – the one with the black and yellow plastic handle – and screwed a hasp and staple combination into both sides of the door, so the apartment could be secured from inside and out.

While doing this, he finished the bottle of whiskey.

Sleep did not come that night. He simply lay in bed, turning this way and that, pushing his blanket off him and then pulling it back on, flipping his pillow over repeatedly, his neck kinking, his ankles popping, his right arm falling asleep as he crushed it under the weight of his body, then his left. Thoughts swirled round his brain, which refused to go silent.

After what felt like an eternity – would this useless fucking night never end? – the gray light of morning began to seep in past the edges of the blue blanket nailed over the window.

The alarm clock didn't have a chance to ring. He shut it off early, got out of bed, and padded to the bathroom.

He brushed his teeth and spat toothpaste and blood into the basin. He rinsed it down the drain, then cupped his hand under the running water, brought a palmful to his mouth, swished it around in there, and spat again. He turned off the water and stared at himself in the mirror, his face only inches from the glass. He looked into his own green eyes – green with flecks of brown. He had tiny bumps under his eyes, just above his cheekbones. They were white and about the size of the tip of a pen. He had accidentally scratched a few off once when he had an itch and despite their size they bled quite a bit. He pushed on the gray bag under his left eye. It was soft and moist and when he pushed on his eyeball through it his eye made a squeaking noise, as air was forced from a duct there, and his vision went blurry. He scraped the eye boogers from the corners of his eyes with a fingernail. He looked at them and then wiped his finger on his pajamas.

Then he turned away from the mirror and looked at the corpse lying in the now almost ice-free bathtub. He should have bought more ice yesterday. He would have to buy more this morning, even if it meant being late for work. He walked to the tub and sat on the edge of it. The porcelain was cool through his pajamas.

'You had a very beautiful wife,' he said. 'I hope you appreciated her.'

He reached down and grabbed the corpse's cold purple hand. The skin was soft and loose on the bones, like the skin on an undercooked chicken. He pulled the ring off the third finger and skin came with it, turning inside out and peeling backwards. Simon rinsed the gold band off under the faucet before putting it on his own finger. Then he sat back down beside the corpse. It was just beginning to smell. The scent was thick and slightly sweet. You could feel it like horseradish behind the roof of your mouth and the backs of your eyes.

'Me,' he said, 'I've never been in love before. I've often wondered what it felt like. So many poems and songs try to describe it, it must be—' He stopped there, licking his lips. He just didn't know how to finish the sentence.

With most of the ice gone, he could see the corpse's right hand. It was a blue-white color, the color of a week-old bruise, and covered in a network of scabbed-over cuts.

Strange.

He got to his feet and walked out of the bathroom.

He was only fifteen minutes late for work, and only three times that morning did he stop working in order to look at the gold band on the third finger of his left hand. When he did stop, he held his hand palm up and looked down at it, and with his right hand he twisted the ring around and around on his finger, thinking of what it meant to be attached to someone by such a thing. He longed for that. But then each moment passed – he snapped himself from his thoughts – and he went back to work.

*

He walked into the diner with his grease-stained lunch bag hanging from his fist. Robert and Chris had left without him again. He stood on the scarred vinyl floor and scanned the room, looking for his friends. The diner was busy, full of chatter and the sounds of forks and knives scraping against plates, and chairs being scooted in or pushed out, and heads of blond and brown and black and red hair filled Simon's view. But after a moment Simon saw Robert's ponytail hanging down his back. Robert and Chris were sitting side by side in a booth in the back corner. Their backs were to the door. It was almost as if they were hoping Simon wouldn't see them.

Simon weaved his way through the crowded tables and sat down across from them. Their food had already arrived and they were eating.

'Hi, guys.'

'Hi,' Chris said.

Robert did not look up from his plate. He simply dragged a couple fries through a smear of ketchup and shoved them into his mouth.

'How you doing, Robert?'

'I'm okay,' Robert said, his voice cold. 'I just lost my appetite, though.' He did not look up at Simon when he spoke. He simply stared down at his plate.

Simon blinked. Then he understood what Robert had meant last night about no longer owing him anything, what he meant when he said they were square.

'Oh,' he said after a minute. 'Okay.'

Chris looked confused. 'Okay, what?' he said through a mouthful of food.

Simon didn't answer. He got to his feet and walked toward an empty table. As he did the sound of Chris asking Robert what was going on faded into the overall noise in the room and became inaudible. Simon sat down. He unpacked his lunch and ate without even tasting his food, just giving fuel to the machine that was his body, just doing what was necessary. His stomach did not feel good. He glanced at Robert and Chris a couple times, but they were simply eating and talking and did not look back. Not even Chris.

Maybe it was best this way. As long as Robert stayed quiet it probably was.

When his lunch was gone he folded up the cling wrap in which it had been packaged, making several small translucent squares and stacking them neatly on the table. Then he folded his grease-stained lunch bag into quarters and put it in the inside pocket of his corduroy sport coat.

He got to his feet.

Alone on his couch with a glass of whiskey in his hands. The glass was cold and wet with condensation. Skip James was singing 'Hard Time Killin' Floor Blues', and Simon was staring at his grayish reflection in the broken television in the corner. He'd turned it on when he got home, but there was no picture, just sound, so he'd turned it off again.

He finished his whiskey and set the glass down on the coffee table. He looked at the photograph of Samantha and Jeremy Shackleford and twisted the wedding band on his hand. He liked the pressure of it on the webs between his fingers. He liked the weight of it. He imagined himself in that photograph. He imagined himself caressing Samantha's body. He imagined himself making love with her, feeling her hot exhalations as she breathed into the crook of his neck.

He poured himself another drink.

Once he'd decided what he was going to do he felt okay. He slept soundly. If he dreamed at all, the dreams were peaceful, and he awoke the next morning feeling better than he had in a very long time, despite the dull ache of a hangover hovering around his head like a cloud, despite the sourness in his stomach.

The office was Saturday quiet, staffed at ten per cent, and in the quiet all Simon could think about was what he was going to do once his shift ended. It was the first time he had ever regretted his six-day work weeks, the only time he would rather have had the day off. Before today he had only regretted the fact that he couldn't also work Sundays.

Eventually, though, it was time to leave.

*

Instead of continuing along Wilshire to the Filboyd Apartments, Simon made a right onto Vermont, drove past Sixth, and made a left into the Walgreens parking lot. He pulled into a spot, pushed open the car door, and stepped out onto the asphalt and right into a pink wad of bubblegum. As he walked, he dragged his right foot along the ground, trying to scrape the gum off the bottom of his shoe. By the time he reached the front of the store with its automatic glass doors – a kid standing there trying to sell candy bars from a cardboard box – his foot was barely sticking to the ground at all.

He stepped past the kid, shaking his head, no, I don't want a candy bar, and into the bright fluorescent light of the store. A security guard sat just to the right of the door in a metal fold-out chair – eyeballing him.

Simon hated security guards. There was something about their mere presence that made him feel guilty. He also felt guilty when he heard a siren, momentarily certain that it was the police coming for him – coming to take him away. His heart would start beating fast and his mouth would go dry and he would try to figure out what it was he had done. His mind would flip through all the nasty, horrible thoughts he'd had recently (stupid bitch, someone should—), flip through them like index cards (if I had a knife, I'd—), as he tried to figure out which one he'd acted upon. He must have acted upon one of them: the police were coming for him. Inevitably, the police car screamed past, or it was a fire engine, or it was an ambulance.

Nobody even glanced in his direction. But the guilt still sat there – weighing on him.

Maybe it was simply the built-up guilt of his youthful petty crimes. When he was young he had been quite a thief. He had grown up poor, and the only way for him to get things he wanted was to steal them. He remembered stopping into a convenience store when he was ten or eleven – this was in Austin, Texas, where he had spent his youth – and seeing a box of kites near the back of the store. He looked through them for several minutes, examining the small pictures on their packaging, pictures which were supposed to be depictions of what they would look like in flight – eagles and jet planes and flaming rockets.

'You gonna buy one of them or just gawk?'

'Sorry,' he said, and left the store.

But the next morning on his way to school he had walked into the convenience store with a pronounced limp – apparently he'd injured his knee and couldn't bend it – knowing what he was going to do, and when the guy behind the counter wasn't looking he slid a kite down the leg of his pants and limped right back out. He was sweaty and full of turmoil inside – guilt – but even then he knew the trick to stealing was to not have a guilty expression on the outside, so he made sure his face was calm – bored even – until he was safe.

He'd flown that kite every weekend for two months, until it finally got caught in a tree in Big Stacy Park and he couldn't get it out again.

Maybe it had just been the built-up guilt of his youth before – but this time the guilt was earned, wasn't it? The reason for it decomposing in his bathtub.

He grabbed a basket from the stack sitting between the security guard and the newspaper display case and walked through the store. He collected a box of brown hair dye, a box of razor blades, band-aids, a bottle of alcohol, a bottle of peroxide, and a bag of cotton balls.

Before going to the checkout line, he stopped to look at the paperback novels. He flipped through a couple, sticking his face into one and inhaling its scent before putting it back down again, but he didn't buy one. He didn't read very much any more, but in his youth books had been his only escape from his adoptive father, who was always drunk and as likely to punch him in the face for some imagined offense as hand him a beer and let him stay up late watching television with him. He felt an odd, bittersweet nostalgia whenever he smelled a certain kind of glue used on some paperback novels – or maybe it was the paper itself, or the ink – and when he did, he couldn't help but put his face into the pages and breathe it in. Sometimes he bought a book for that reason alone, whether he was interested in the content or not. Not today, though. Today he had other things on his mind.

He walked into his apartment with a plastic bag hanging from his fist. He set it on the couch and padlocked his door. Then he removed his jacket and his button-up, stripping down to his yellow-pitted T-shirt. He picked up the bag again and walked down the hallway to the bathroom.

He blew into the powder-covered latex gloves and then slipped his hands into them one at a time before lacing his fingers together and forcing them down tight. His stomach felt sour and his liver hurt. He mixed the hair dye in a small plastic bottle and then squirted it through a nozzle onto his gray head of hair. He massaged it into his scalp with gloved fingers, wiping it away with toilet paper when it ran down his forehead or the backs of his ears or his neck. It made his scalp tingle. In ten minutes his head was covered in a brown layer of dye the consistency of warm mayonnaise.

He sat on the toilet and waited, wishing he had bought a book after all. He had a few lying around the apartment, but he'd read them all – most of them more than once. He felt tickles of moisture on the back of his neck and blindly wiped at them with wads of toilet paper. Stomach acid bubbled up into the back of his throat and he swallowed it down again.

Half an hour passed.

He rinsed his head in the basin, under steaming hot water, knowing this was stupid, knowing he couldn't possibly look as much like Jeremy Shackleford as he seemed to at first glance, knowing that even if he did look that much like him he would still never be able to pass himself off as the man.

But then he asked himself, Why not – why couldn't I?

What better way to find out why Shackleford had broken into his apartment and tried to kill him than to give himself access to the man's life?

He thought of the cracks in his ceiling.

He thought of himself floating through space – directionless.

Well, now he had a direction, didn't he? It gave him a sense of purpose, a reason to wake in the morning. There was a mystery in his life, and no matter what it revealed, it had to be better than eight hours at the office, masturbating in a small booth in a pornographic book store, and sleeping on a small mattress while the sounds of the city echoed through his apartment and small insects nibbled at him. It had to be better than that same routine day in and day out as the months fell off the calendar like dead leaves.

Anything would be better than that – anything at all.

Simon pulled his head out of the sink, dried off with a threadbare brown towel. He put his glasses back on and looked at himself in the mirror. He looked like a different person. He felt like a different person.

'Not too bad.'

He peeled the latex gloves off his now sweaty hands –

fingertips white and pruned – and threw them into the trash can.

But he wasn't done yet.

He reached into the plastic bag and pulled out a white and blue box. He opened the paper lid, revealing the shining backs of two hundred razor blades. He slid one of them from the box and held it up close to his eye. He looked past the blade and to his reflection in the peeling medicine cabinet mirror.

Can you do it, Simon?

He swallowed.

'Yes,' he said.

He put the razor blade against his right cheekbone. It was cold and sharp. He exhaled, began to press the blade into his pockmarked skin – and then stopped. He wanted this to be right.

He set the blade down on the counter beside the basin and walked over to the bathtub.

He pulled the grocery bag off the corpse's head, and immediately looked away, gagging. It had only been three days and he had tried to keep the body cold, but already there were things living in the corpse. There was a disturbing subcutaneous movement, as if on the other side of the flesh were a million crawling legs trying to inch the face down the front of the skull.

Simon could not see what he needed to see without turning the head toward him, but he didn't want to touch it. He walked over to the trash can and put one of the gloves back on. When he found himself standing in front of the corpse again, he swallowed, held his breath, and then leaned down and turned the head so he could see the scar. It was four inches long and ran jaggedly from cheekbone to chinbone. It was white, and despite the five o'clock shadow covering the rest of Shackleford's face, it was smooth and free of hair.

He stared at the scar for a long time, ignoring the sucking wet holes the eyes had become, and once he thought he had it etched into his memory, he nodded to himself and turned back to the mirror. He could do this.

Once again, he put the blade against his cheekbone. He breathed heavily, in and out and in and out, almost to the point of hyperventilation, and then he stopped breathing altogether. He pushed the blade down into his cheek, hard, and it forced the skin down with it – the skin taking a surprising amount of pressure – and then there was a popping sound as the skin broke. A bead of blood formed around the corner of the blade. He pushed down further, feeling the skin part. The bead became a stream. Warm liquid flooded down the side of his face. The pain was citric and overwhelming, but he tried to ignore it and simply dragged the blade down his cheek, following his mental image of the corpse's scar.

When he reached the center of the cheek, the blade broke clean through and he ended up cutting his gums as well, and he cursed and stomped on the floor and had to stop. He put the brown towel against his cheek and found himself bent over at the waist, groaning. He tongued the wound on the inside of his mouth. The tip of his tongue touched the towel on the other side. He breathed through his nostrils like an angry bull about to charge. He walked in a circle. The blood continued to pour out of him, and it continued to fill his mouth. He let it drain from between his lips, down his chin, and onto the floor.

'Oh, fuck,' he said through gritted teeth as the taste of metal filled his mouth, warm and thick and salty. He'd cut too deep – far too deep.

After a while, he stood up again.

Still holding the towel against his face, he looked at himself in the mirror. His eyes were red and full of tears. He pulled the towel away and blood poured out of him and dripped onto his T-shirt and splattered on the tile floor and ran along the grout lines like branching rivers. He put the towel back. If he was going to go through with this he had another two inches to go. He'd only managed to cut halfway down his cheek. He wasn't done.

He looked around for the razor blade. He'd dropped it or thrown it or something. When the pain hit – when he broke through the skin of the cheek and cut his own gums – he'd no longer been altogether present. He scanned the countertop and saw nothing but splatters and drips of blood. Then he saw it on the floor, in the corner, amongst a wad of hair and dust which had collected by the bathtub.

He picked it up and threw it into the trash can. It

clinked as it hit the edge and then disappeared amongst the paper waste.

There were a hundred and ninety-nine clean ones; there was no point in risking infection.

After sliding a clean blade from the box, he pulled the towel away from his cheek. Blood still seeped from the wound, but it was no longer pouring out of him.

He tongued the wound, saw a glimpse of it through the cheek. It made his stomach feel sour.

He closed his eyes, trying not to be sick (and trying not to wonder what kind of pain that would produce in his new wound), and once the nausea passed – it rolled through his stomach, and he burped, tasting acid, then swallowed it away – he opened them again. It had been difficult the first time; this time it felt impossible. He knew what pain he had to look forward to – the sharpest of it was still fresh in his mind, only moments old. Before it had merely been an idea. Now it was a reality. He knew the pain. He did not want more of it. But he thought, too, he was past the point of changing his mind. He was scarred for life; he might as well finish doing what he had set out to do. He put the blade against the edge of the wound. It stung before he even went to work. His stomach clenched. He felt dizziness swim over him. When he looked at himself in the mirror he felt that he was looking at a stranger.

He closed his eyes, gritted his teeth – his jaw going tight and cramping with the pressure of it – and sawed the blade down toward his chin. As he cut downward, his head seemed to roll out of consciousness, like a ball on a gentle slope – and then it dropped off the edge into total darkness.

He woke up on the bathroom floor. His mouth was full of blood both clotted and wet. He sat up, tongued his cheek, felt the sting of pain, and smiled. The movement of facial muscles sent more electric pain throbbing through his face and neck. Blood was still drizzling from the side of his cheek. He looked down at his wrinkled white T-shirt. It was covered in a thick, drying crust of burgundy. His glasses – also splattered with blood – were on the floor by the edge of the counter. He picked them up and put them back onto his face. Out-of-focus blood spots covered the lenses. He pushed himself up off the cold tile floor and onto his feet. He looked at himself in the mirror. The reflection he saw was something out of a horror film. It looked like he'd just spent the last hour rolling around a slaughterhouse floor.

He got a washcloth from one of the drawers and wetted it with hot water and gently wiped at his face and neck. Even though he started far from the wound, it hurt to wipe the blood away. His nerve endings felt raw and exposed. Still he continued, rinsing and wiping, being careful not to actually wipe at the slit in his face.

Once he'd gotten most of the blood away, he started dabbing at the wound itself with cotton balls soaked in peroxide, watching the peroxide turn white with bubbles. It stung, but not as badly as the alcohol would, and that was next.

After unwrapping a dozen band-aids, Simon taped them over the wound, thinking that he should have purchased gauze and medical tape instead. He hadn't anticipated the extent of the damage that would be done – that now was done. The first layer of band-aids immediately went red and he stuck on a second layer, and then a third.

He found an expired bottle of Vicodin in the back of the medicine cabinet. He couldn't remember ever having been prescribed Vicodin, and, in fact, he still wasn't certain he ever had been. Maybe the last tenant had left the pills. He couldn't know: the name had been peeled off the label. But there had been a few sweaters in the bedroom closet, and a few frying pans in the kitchen, and of course that dead ficus on the fire escape, so it was possible. He didn't care. Even expired, its usefulness fading with age, it should dull the pain better than acetaminophen. He swallowed two of the pills, and then undressed, leaving his bloody clothes in a pile on the floor – he would take care of the clean-up tomorrow; right now, the entire right side of his head was throbbing like a bad tooth – and padded to the bedroom. He crawled under his blanket and looked up at the cracked ceiling.

He wondered if this had been a mistake.

Throughout most of the night he was awake and in pain. Once, as morning approached, he fell asleep with his eyes open and dreamed the bedroom was filling up with water. He dreamed – with his eyes open – that he was drowning. Then the dream – or the hallucination, whatever it was – was over, and he was simply lying in his bed again. He was covered in sweat and the night air was chilling him.

He closed his eyes, but sleep didn't come again.

He stumbled into the living room early next morning. It was Sunday. He had cleaned up himself and the bathroom and was wearing a pair of brown checkered pants and a T-shirt and his corduroy jacket. He walked to the couch and sat down. He bent down and picked up the phone from the floor and set it in his lap. He dialed seven digits. After three rings the automated answering machine picked up and he dialed a three-digit extension, followed by the pound key. It being Sunday, he thought he would just leave a message, but someone picked up.

'Hello.'

'Hello – Mr Thames?'

'Speaking.'

'It's Simon Johnson.'

'Yes?'

'Yes.'

'Is something the matter, Simon?'

'Oh. I'm just calling to let you know I won't be in next week. I've had a death in the family. My mother. Well, my adoptive mother. I was adopted. I don't know if you knew that. Anyways, I'll be flying down to Austin for the funeral and to be with my family.'

'I'm awfully sorry,' Mr Thames said.

'Okay.'

Simon pulled the phone away from his ear.

'Simon?'

The tinny sound of the voice barely reached him, but it did, and he put the phone to his ear once more.

'Yes, sir?'

'I know this is a bad time for you, but is there a number where we can contact you if we have any questions about your accounts?'

'You can call my apartment. I'll check the messages daily.'

'Okay, Simon.'

'Okay.'

He put the telephone back into its cradle and set it back onto the floor. He didn't have an answering machine.

*

Later that afternoon he drove downtown to the Los Angeles Central Library on Fifth and Grand. He parked on Fifth Street, across from the Edison building, stepped from his car, took one last drag from his cigarette, and dropped it into the metal tray which lined the top of the trash can out front. The tray was filled with nicotine-yellow water and cigarette butts and straw wrappers and wads of bubblegum and bubblegum papers. The cigarette Simon dropped in sizzled briefly and then went silent. His cheek was covered in multiple layers of band-aids. Inside his mouth, though, a slow flow of blood still oozed from the wound when he made any kind of expression at all, and when he smoked it stung. But he wasn't going to stop smoking. Had he any will he would have stopped long before now. He spit a wad of blood into the trash can and headed for the front door, past a homeless guy with no shoes whose toes looked black with decay.

He walked into the lobby, where a line was twisting toward the checkout desk, filled with people holding library-card applications and library cards and stacks of books to check in, or out, or both.

After examining a floor plan of the library by the escalators – he'd only ever gone upstairs to where they kept fiction and literature – he found what he was looking for two floors below ground, on lower level two, in the science and technology section. He walked past the information desk and made a left, and there he found the mathematics books.

He grabbed an armload of them, almost at random, and then found an unoccupied wooden cubicle and sat down. He opened one of the books. It told him that if velocity was constant, and one knew the velocity, then distance was that multiplied by time, and if one knew the time and the distance, then one could figure out the velocity, but if one knew only one of the three variables, one was, ultimately, fucked.

He wondered how often in life – rather than in hypothetical situations – one really had enough information to know anything with any amount of certainty.

There was an entire chapter in the same book dedicated to spheres. He had some experience with spheres. He lived on one, for instance – on an approximation of one, anyway. Here was a fact about the sphere that the book didn't discuss: the sphere offered no escape: go in any direction for any distance, for an eternity, and you would never find the edge. You might cover the same ground a thousand times – but you would never find an edge.

Time passed.

*

It was four days after Simon's first trip to the library that he took the band-aids off for the first time. They had started to smell bad. He had been tonguing the wound from the inside since the beginning and had felt it growing shallower as its lips began to seal themselves together. Now he wanted to see how it was progressing on the outside. He peeled the band-aids away with some pain – his beard was growing in and the adhesive was sticking to it – and in a few minutes the crescent scab was revealed. It was brownish-red and about an eighth of an inch wide at its widest point and ran four inches in length. There were strange little stretch marks in his skin at the edges of the wound, and it was red and raw there as well, but he didn't think it was infected. Each end of the wound, where the cut had been shallowest, was already mostly healed. The scab had peeled away there, revealing pink scar. The middle, though, was still deep and raw. If he grimaced or frowned or smiled it bled still through cracks in the scab. But it was looking good. It was healing well. In another week or two the scab would flake away, revealing a scar very much like the one on the face of the – now stinking – corpse in his bathtub. Simon glanced at it. He was going to have to do something with it. He was tired of driving through the city, hunting for ice. He was going to have to get rid of it.

But not yet. He was afraid that if he got rid of it, someone would find it, and this ruse would be over before it was fairly begun. If it was here, it was safe. And he was safe. If it was out in the world, then anything might happen.

He put a cotton ball against the open mouth of the peroxide bottle, and then tilted the bottle. He wiped at his face, cleaning old blood away.

After that, alcohol.

And after that, a fresh dozen band-aids.

Soon it would be time. In another week – maybe two.

2

JEREMY

Even though there was parking directly in front of the house, Simon drove to the end of the block – about six houses down – before pulling his Volvo to the curb and killing the engine. His right cheek was free of band-aids now and lined with a meaty white scar. There was still a bit of pink where the wound hadn't completely healed, but he couldn't make himself wait any longer. He'd just been sitting around thinking about it for days.

He knew more about mathematics than he ever had before.

He tongued at his cheek. There were a dozen hairs growing on the inside. When the wound healed it healed with hair follicles in the pink interior of his mouth and they had begun growing hairs that made the lining of his cheek itch.

He tongued at the centimeter-long hairs as he stepped from his car, and then slammed the door shut. He had become aware of the hair growing in his mouth six days ago, but on the drive over it had become an obsession, despite what he was doing here this morning. He reached into his mouth with his left hand and grabbed one of them between his thumb and index finger – pinching it against the pad of the finger with the thumbnail – and yanked.

There was a sharp sting and his eyes watered and he tasted blood. He looked at the small gray hair for a moment – examining it closely, the way it curled and formed a half circle, the white pin-dot of flesh hanging on one end – and then tossed it away.

He tongued at his cheek again, but then forced himself to stop. He wasn't thinking about it despite what he was doing here this morning; he was thinking about it *because* of what he was doing here this morning. He was distracting himself from it. But it served no end. There was no profit in it.

He turned away from his car and walked toward the Shackleford house. He could see Samantha's Mercedes sitting in the driveway.

Soon he would know if she believed him.

'Hey, Jeremy. Got that hammer you borrowed?'

Simon paused. He was standing on the first step leading up to the front porch. When the morning breeze blew he could smell basil and rosemary on the air. The pollen in the purple flowers on the front porch made his eyes water and his nose run. The voice came from behind him – the voice of a man who ate gravel.

Simon swallowed and turned around.

A heavy man in his late forties was jogging in place about ten feet away on the sidewalk. He wore stained gray sweatpants and a T-shirt that didn't quite cover his light-bulb-shaped belly. Between his sweats and his shirt, a white slice of hairy gut. He had a face like wet papier-mâché, drooping off the bones, and his neck was dotted with razor bumps. A few white bits of toilet paper were stuck to his skin with drops of drying blood. Simon's adoptive father used to call those red-dotted bits of toilet paper Japanese flags. As in, 'You got a Japanese flag stuck to your neck there, pal.'

He had been dead for six years now. Simon hadn't gone to the funeral, but after his mom told him about it – that the old man had been found dead in his motor home in Nevada (they were divorced when Simon was fifteen) – he'd spent two weeks walking around in a daze. He hadn't cried. He hadn't even felt particularly sad, but he felt some-thing related to sadness, something that lived next door to it, a kind of echoing hollow. A month later he cried about it for the first and last time. It was strange. He hadn't liked the man – in fact, he had hated him – but he was the only father Simon knew and he'd loved him too.

'What's that?' he said.

'My hammer. You got it?'

'Oh, yeah,' he said. 'It's in my garage. Mind if I bring it by later? I'm kinda busy.'

'Yeah, no prob. I can't take it now anyway. About to go on a run. I just saw you and thought I'd toss out a reminder.'

'Oh,' Simon said. 'Okay. I'll bring it by later.'

'Sounds good. See you then.'

'Right.'

The man turned and jogged a few steps before stopping and backing up again.

'By the way – what happened to your face?'

'My face?'

'That scar.'

Simon touched his cheek.

'Oh, that. My barber had a seizure.'

The man was silent a moment.

'Really?'

Simon nodded.

The guy whistled, sucking in through his teeth. 'Tough luck.'

'You're telling me.'

'Okay. Later, then.'

'Later.'

The guy went on with his jog.

Simon watched him go, letting out a relieved sigh: one person had believed him to be Jeremy Shackleford, anyway.

But what had he meant mentioning the scar? Hadn't Shackleford had one just like it?

He pushed quietly through the front door and walked down the hallway. He felt sick to his stomach. Despite having brushed his teeth, the dry slab of his tongue tasted awful. He swallowed, or tried to, but had no spit.

At the bedroom door he stopped. It was cracked a bit, and he could hear the sound of shallow breathing – the shallow breathing of sleep, one long sigh followed by another – and he could smell the clean smell of a woman's sweat and the stale smell of slept-on sheets. He put his hand up, pressed his fingers against the coarse grain of the wood, straightened them till his knuckles were locked, and pushed. The door opened easily, sliding gently against the plush wool bedroom carpet and then stopping, leaving behind a half circle of nap it had brushed flat, like the wing of a snow angel.

Samantha was asleep on the bed. She was lying on striped burgundy sheets, beneath a white quilt, her head resting on one pillow, her arms wrapped around another, hugging it in place of a human absence – which absence, Simon thought, was in his bathtub. Well, some of it was. Once the smell had gotten too bad to tolerate, once neighbors started calling Leonard and complaining about a foul stench, once he had given up on burning incense and icing the body, he had driven to the store and picked up a half dozen bottles of drain cleaner. He poured the drain cleaner over the corpse, let it dissolve the tissue, and ran warm shower water over it. He did this four days in a row (going to a different store each time). The drain had clogged several times, but he'd managed to plunge the stoppages through. Now what was left was mostly bones and teeth and what hair hadn't swirled down the drain. He still had to get rid of that, but he was afraid. Dental records and so on. He would have to smash out the teeth and—

That was for later.

He walked to the bed and stood over Samantha. Samantha was for now.

She was pale and smooth and beautiful.

He had to make her believe that he was Jeremy Shackleford.

When he sat on the edge of the bed a low moan escaped her throat. He reached a hand out and brushed the back of it across her smooth cheek, feeling the light blonde hairs on it like the fuzz on a peach. He ran the pad of a thumb across her soft lips. His breathing grew heavier. He swallowed.

Yes, Samantha was for now.

He imagined lying with her, loving her. He imagined her loving him in return. It seemed like a dream. Would she know he wasn't Jeremy? There were so many things besides appearance that made a man – the way he closed his eyes when angry, forcing himself to calm down; the way he bit at his bottom lip; the way he carried himself when he walked – and marriages, Simon thought, were so intimate that it would be impossible for a spouse not to, eventually, pick up on all of them. Twins, for instance, might look identical to strangers, but parents and spouses could tell the difference in an instant. Would she be able to see he wasn't Jeremy just as quickly? Would she look at him and just know? Would all this have been pointless?

There was only one way to find out.

'Samantha.'

She rolled over in her sleep, mumbling something under her breath.

He reached out and ran fingers through her hair.

'Samantha.'

She brushed his hand away.

'Not right now, Jeremy,' she said, still asleep. But a moment later her eyes opened. 'Jeremy?'

She sat up and there was something like fear on her face, her eyes wide and blue and beautiful, and her mouth was hanging open, and she crawled backwards, away from him, until she bumped up against the dark wood headboard.

'Jeremy?'

'Hi.'

'Where – where have you been?'

'I – I don't know.'

'You don't – did you have another?' She pinched her eyes closed and rubbed at them, still mostly asleep, apparently incapable of grasping completely what was happening when only a moment earlier she had been dreaming impossible dreams. She opened her eyes again. 'Did you have another – spell?'

'I guess I must have.'

Had Shackleford had blackouts as well? Simon's had been less and less frequent (six months ago he was having them often, but now they almost never came), but just a couple of days before all this started – before Shackleford broke into his apartment – he'd found himself in the adult book store and didn't know how he'd gotten there, couldn't remember it at all. He was wearing only one shoe. When he got back to his apartment, he'd found the other shoe sitting on his coffee table. What did it mean that—

Suddenly Samantha was crying. At first Simon didn't know what was happening – she simply looked down at her lap, and a moment later her body began to shake and hair that had been tucked behind her small but jutting ears – flopped out like loose shutters – fell into her face and small sobs escaped her – and even after he did know what was happening he didn't know what to do. He simply sat and stared at her as she shook and looked down at her own lap.

'It's okay,' he said. 'I'm back. It's me – Jeremy.'

She looked up at him with her red-rimmed eyes and wiped at her cheeks and her nose with the back of her hand. She tucked loose strands of hair back behind her ears. Her eyes were alive with emotion and beautiful for it. But as she searched his face, something behind them changed somehow. Something entered her eyes that Simon didn't like at all.

'You're not – who are you?'

Simon swallowed. His face got hot with blood but he tried not to show it, tried only to give Samantha a dead-pan while he thought of what to say next. Like stealing a kite, half the trick was not to give yourself away.

'Who am I?' he said with absolutely false humor. 'Jeremy.' He said this in the same tone he'd use to explain to someone that the sky was blue: it was so obvious it didn't deserve mentioning.

'No,' she said. 'You're not.'

'Don't be ridiculous.'

She shook her head.

The way a man held his shoulders, the way his mouth looked when he was relaxed, how often he blinked while lying or telling the truth, where he rested his hands – in his pockets or on his lap or pressed against his hips – the way he scratched his face, whether he crossed his legs at the ankles or knees or not at all when sitting down: a man was more than his appearance. He should have known he could never get away with this. He had known, hadn't he?

He licked his lips.

He had to make her believe. She hadn't seen him for weeks. Her memories of him weren't fresh. He could make her believe. He had to.

'Why?' he said, then cleared his throat and swallowed. His tongue was sticking to the roof of his mouth. 'Why would you say that?' He smiled. 'Who else would I be, sugar bear?'

She returned his smile then, only hers was real. Had he stumbled upon a correct phrase when he called her sugar bear? He thought he must have. He swallowed and then smiled again. This time his was real too.

'There's my sugar bear,' he said.

She reached out and touched the scar curving down his face from cheekbone to chinbone. She traced the pad of a finger across it.

'What happened?'

'What do you mean?'

'Your face.'

'Accident,' he said, guessing. 'You remember.'

She shook her head.

'I remember twenty-five thousand dollars in surgeries to have it removed,' she said. 'What have you done to yourself?'

'I don't . . .'

He shook his head.

'Goddamn it,' she said.

She appeared to be on the verge of tears again, but then she looked away, blinked several times, and swallowed. It passed. She had the weary and ragged look of a woman who had suffered her husband's insanity for a long time. Simon hadn't seen it on her before, but he saw it now. The tired eyes, the set jaw.

He'd been insane. She had loved Jeremy Shackleford,

but he had been mad. Maybe that was all there was to Shackleford wanting him dead. Maybe Shackleford had seen him on the street and their similar appearance had been enough to send him over the edge. It could be that simple, couldn't it?

There was no rule that said things had to be complex. Didn't Occam's razor even state the opposite, that the simplest answer was usually the correct one – that you should cut away all that was superfluous?

But *was* that an answer? Simon wasn't sure.

'Why are you wearing your old glasses?' Samantha said.

'I don't know,' he said.

She grabbed his face in both her hands and looked at him and said 'Goddamn it' again, and then she pulled his face to hers and kissed his hair and his cheeks and his chin and his mouth and his neck.

'Goddamn it.'

'I'm sorry.'

'I know,' she said. 'You're always sorry.'

'I'm sorry for that, too.'

'I know,' she said. 'Let's get you into a bath. You smell like you haven't had one in weeks.'

Simon stood barefoot on the cold tile floor. The bathtub was running hot water, and Samantha had put soap into it, so there was now a mountain of foam just beneath the faucet – a reverse volcano into which water was rushing. Steam rose off the liquid's surface.

'Do you remember anything?'

Simon shook his head. He thought it was best if he remembered nothing. If he had nothing to say he was less likely to say the wrong thing, to give himself away.

Samantha pulled his corduroy coat off and hung it on a brass hook poking from the door, and then unbuttoned his shirt and pulled it off him.

'I thought you donated all these clothes to Good Will.'

'I – I boxed them up, but I never drove them over.'

Samantha unbuttoned his pants and shoved them down his legs. They piled at his feet and he stepped out of them. He had hairy white legs covered in skin like a plucked chicken, thin hair except at the knees, which his pants had rubbed bare, and thin calves lined with blue veins.

'Get in the tub,' she said. 'I'll scrub you down.'

He walked to the bathtub and stepped his right foot into the water. At first he couldn't tell whether it was hot or cold – the shock had confused his body – but after a moment his nerves were reoriented, and he yanked his scalded foot back out, sucking in air through his teeth.

'Don't be a baby. Get in.'

Simon tried a second time, going easily, first one foot and then the other. He stood still a moment, letting his body adjust, and then lowered himself in slowly, hands gripping either side of the tub. He was all right until his scrotum touched the water, and then he stood up again, or tried, but couldn't manage it before Samantha pushed him back down. His skin turned pink.

He kept waiting for Samantha to see some scar or birthmark on his body that Jeremy didn't have, or to notice the absence of a scar or birthmark, but neither of those things happened.

Samantha grabbed a dry loofah from the edge of the tub, soaked it in the water, squeezed it out, and scrubbed Simon's back.

'How did you get home?'

'What do you mean?'

'Your car's been in the garage.'

'Oh, right.'

'So?'

'I took the train,' he said, despite the fact that he had never used the city's public transportation system. He had seen the tracks near Union Station, and occasionally saw one of the light rail trains rolling to or from Pasadena, and every once in a while walked over subway grating on the sidewalk, in Hollywood and Koreatown, but he'd never actually ridden one of the city's trains, or even one of its busses. Still, it was the first thing that came to mind, and it seemed to do the job – Samantha asked no more questions.

She scrubbed at his back silently for a couple minutes.

'My show's tonight.'

'Your show?'

'My exhibition. My paintings.'

'Oh.'

'I have to go. Gil's been planning it for weeks.'

'Okay.'

'What do you want to do?'

'I'll stay home if you want.'

'I don't feel comfortable leaving you home alone.'

'Then I'll come with you.'

'Do you think you'll be okay? I know you hate crowds, and on top of everything else—'

'I'll be okay.'

'Sure?'

He nodded.

Samantha bent down and kissed the back of his head.

'Okay. Now wet your hair.'

Then she shoved his head down, forcing it underwater.

There were still beads of water dotting his naked back, and his clean underwear was spotted with moisture. He stood in front of his side of the closet – Jeremy Shackleford's side of the closet – looking at ten suits, five of them gray, three black, one brown, one dark green. They were hanging on wooden hangers, and they were all facing in the same direction. To their right, about a dozen dry-cleaned white shirts. To the right of the shirts, cardigan sweaters in various colors, about half of them plaid. And at the end of the closet, a tie rack with at least a dozen silk ties hanging from it, each facing out so that Simon – Jeremy – could examine the patterns and pick which one he wanted. On a shelf above all this, several white T-shirts – no yellow sweat stains in the pits of these – folded and stacked neatly.

Simon grabbed one of the T-shirts off the shelf and slipped into it. It took a bit of effort because the moisture on his body clung to the fabric, but soon enough he had it on. He grabbed the brown suit and pulled the pants off the hanger, tossing the jacket to the mattress behind him. He slipped into them, wondering how they would fit. They were a bit big around the waist – which was nothing a cinched belt couldn't fix – but otherwise the fit was nice.

Samantha walked in wearing a paint-splattered pair of jeans and a T-shirt. She was carrying two cups of coffee. She handed him one of the cups and the warmth of the porcelain against the palms of his hands felt good.

'Thank you.'

He sipped his coffee. She'd prepared it just how he liked – lots of milk, no sugar.

'You're still wearing those glasses.'

'Yeah.'

'Well, I hate them.'

'Oh.'

'Please don't wear them.'

'Okay.'

'There's contact lenses in the medicine cabinet. I checked.'

'Okay.'

He sipped his coffee again, and then set it down on the dresser. He grabbed a white button-up shirt from the closet and put his arms into it and buttoned it, starting at the bottom to make sure the buttons were lined up, and then sliding the rest through their buttonholes and into place. Then he grabbed a green checkered cardigan, put that on, and started looking for a tie.

'Are you going somewhere?'

'I thought I'd go to the college. Do I have a class today?'

Samantha nodded. 'In an hour. You have that one Monday class. The history of geometry or something.'

'It's Monday?'

Samantha nodded. 'But are you sure you're ready to go back to work?'

'I think so.'

'You're okay?'

'I'm fine. I want to get back to work.'

I want to find out why Jeremy Shackleford wanted me dead.

'Howard's been covering your classes. He can cover one more.'

He had no idea who Howard was.

'How many did I miss?'

'Several.'

'Several?'

'A week's worth – six. Classes only started a week ago or you'd've missed more.'

He nodded.

'What did you tell him?'

'Who?'

'Henry.'

'Howard?'

'Howard.'

She paused and there was concern in her eyes. She looked like she might say something about him using the wrong name, but then she didn't. 'I said you'd had an accident and I didn't know when you'd be able to work – and with that fucking scar on your face—' She sighed. 'Anyway, I think everything's okay.'

'Good,' Simon said. 'Thank you.'

Samantha nodded.

'I made you a two o'clock appointment with Dr Zurasky.'

A pulse of pain throbbed just above Simon's left eyebrow and his eye began to water. He pinched his eyes closed, opened them after several blinks, and looked at Samantha.

'How did – how did you know about Zurasky?'

'Of course I know about Zurasky. My sister referred us to him.'

'When?'

Samantha said nothing for a long time. She just stared at him. Then: 'Are you *sure* you should be going to work?'

'I'm fine.'

'You don't seem fine.'

'Well, I am.'

'You don't seem yourself at all.'

'I'm just— When did I start seeing him?'

'You saw him a few times two winters ago, I think, then last June— You know this. I don't know why we're having this conversation.'

'I don't remember.'

'I don't think you should go to work.'

'I'm going.'

'I'm against it.'

'I need to. I don't want to feel like – I don't want to feel like an invalid.'

Samantha bit her lip.

'If you think—'

'I'm fine.'

He took the disposable contact lenses from their boxes in the medicine cabinet, first the right one and then the left. He peeled the foil from the top of the right lens case, being careful not to spill the saline solution, and then got the lens on the pad of his index finger. He examined it a moment to make sure it was right side out and once he was sure it was he held his right eye open with his left hand, and settled the lens gently onto the green of his eye.

He blinked a few times, wiped at the water running down his cheek.

He closed his left eye and looked at his own reflection with his right. It was somewhat blurry, but not as blurry as he had expected it to be, and the blur might be the result of his being unused to wearing contact lenses. He might be able to get away with wearing these despite the fact that the prescription wasn't made for him.

He peeled the foil off the container for the left lens and repeated the process. He blinked both eyes several times. He felt something in his left eye, looked closely at his reflection and thought he saw an eyelash floating around in there, rinsed it out with saline solution, blinked again, wiped the water off his face again, and looked at his own reflection again.

'I'll be goddamned,' he said.

His car was a Saab. At first he thought it was the same Saab that killed the mutt he had fed, but there was no blood on the rear license plate and it didn't look like it had been washed recently. It was covered in a thin coat of grime. Also, Samantha said it had been in the garage. And Jeremy, being dead, couldn't have driven it back here. Death tended to hinder such activity.

He got inside, started the engine, slid the transmission into reverse, and backed out of the garage, careful not to hit Samantha's car, which was parked in the driveway to his

right. He rolled out into the street, put the car into drive –
and drove.

While he drove he thought about what he was doing
and why. Was he really doing this in order to find out why
Shackleford had broken into his apartment – was he really
doing this in order to find out why Shackleford had
wanted him dead? Or was he doing it because Shackleford
had had everything he'd ever wanted, everything he'd
dreamed of but had never attained – because he wanted to
step into a life he'd always desired but which someone else
had built?

'There's no reason it can't be both,' he told himself
while he drove. Shackleford was already dead. Why
shouldn't he step into his place – if he could get away
with it?

Jeremy Shackleford's office was a small rectangular box,
about eight feet wide and ten feet deep. The walls were
roughly textured and one of them – the one to the left of
the oak desk which sat in the middle of the room, facing
the door – was painted green. A captioned picture of
Bertrand Russell hung there. The caption read:

> **It has been said that man is a rational animal.**
> **All my life I have been searching for evidence**
> **which could support this.**

Simon sat at the desk and looked around. He pulled open a drawer and found a pint of whiskey. He unscrewed the whiskey and took a swallow. It burned his throat and felt good and warm inside him.

The clock said he had half an hour before his class started. That gave him some time to search the place. He took another swallow of whiskey, put the bottle back, and started looking.

Fifteen minutes later he walked into the room where he would be teaching. He'd found nothing in the office, but then he had no idea what he should be looking for. Maybe once he knew more he'd know better what to look for. He glanced around the classroom. It did not surprise him to find that it was small – about big enough to hold an algebra class in a high school. This was an arts college, after all; people loved neither their maths nor their sciences at such institutions. He was glad for that. He was pretty sure he could handle teaching the history of geometry to students who were fidgeting and thinking about the short film they were directing or the oil painting they were in the middle of – or whatever – without too much trouble. If he'd had to deal with people who gave a damn about mathematics, it might have been a problem.

He'd stopped at the cafeteria between here and the office and picked up a large cup of coffee, and he sipped it now, looking around the room, at the empty wooden desks with initials carved into them, at the overflowing trash can in the corner, stuffed with donut boxes and orange juice jugs and coffee cups and muffin wrappers from whatever class was here at eight o'clock. Based on the red writing on the whiteboard at the front of the room –

Au resto
Bon marché
Ce n'est pas propre

– Simon guessed first-semester French.

He walked to the whiteboard, used a stained cloth that was hanging from a nail in the wall to wipe the board clean, and then stared at the blank surface, fluorescent light reflecting off it. He exhaled, wondering if he was crazy for doing this. Maybe he was – maybe he *was* crazy – but he had never felt more himself either. Of course, that might be a symptom of his insanity. Probably was.

He turned to face the empty room.

'Today,' he said, 'we'll be discussing the development of geometry in ancient Greece.'

'I already covered that chapter.'

Simon jumped, startled, and turned toward the door.

A man in a plaid yellow suit stood in the doorway. He was in his fifties with a trimmed mustache and white shoes with buckles on them. He was bald on top – the slope of his head shiny enough to see your reflection in – but the hair he had growing around the back and hooked over his ears with sideburns was long and wrapped in a rubberband to form a ponytail. His eyes were brown – except for the whites, which were very red – and cocked up on the inside to give him a permanent look of gentleness regardless of mood. His skin was bad. He wore several bracelets for various causes – he appeared to hate cancer, AIDS, and orphaned children in equal measure.

'How are you, Jeremy?'

'I'm okay, Professor Ullman.'

Simon must have accidentally raised his pitch at the end of the sentence, making it a question, because Professor Ullman said, 'Who else would I be?'

'I wouldn't know.'

'Neither would I, Jeremy.'

'Okay.'

'And since when do you call me Professor Ullman?'

'I'm sorry. Henry.'

Wrong answer. Simon could see it on the man's face. What had Samantha said his name was? Don't panic, just give him a deadpan and maybe he'll let it slide.

But, of course, he didn't.

'What did you call me?'

'What?'

Oh, goddamn it, what did Samantha say his fucking *name* was?

'You called me Henry. Are you sure you're okay to come back?'

'I didn't call you Henry.'

'I heard you, Jeremy.'

'Well, Howard – ' there it was – 'if I did I simply misspoke.'

'You're sure you're okay?'

'Sure I'm sure. I'm fine. I had an accident is all.'

'That's what Samantha said—' Howard put a finger on his own cheekbone and traced an invisible line down to his chin. 'That's what Samantha said, but that doesn't look like an accident to me.'

'What do you mean?'

'I think you know.'

'Well, I don't. And anyways, I'm fine, Howard.'

Howard took several steps closer to Simon, examining him. Simon suddenly understood why his eyes were red and tired-looking. The stench of marijuana clung to his clothes and hung around him in a pungent cloud. You could almost feel it sticking to your skin.

'You just – ' Howard exhaled through his nostrils – 'you don't seem yourself. I look at you and I think: this man isn't Jeremy Shackleford. His face doesn't move quite right, his eyes don't look the same.' He looked away. 'I don't know. Maybe after what happened— Anyway, you're back.' He looked at his watch. 'We'll talk later, and I'll rip out your fucking heart.'

'Excuse me?'

'We'll talk later,' Howard said. 'Your class is about to start.'

*

He sat at the desk at the front of the room as students walked in with backpacks strapped over their shoulders, thumbing cell phones off, listening to music through ear buds, chattering.

He felt nervous and sweaty. Once the class was full – there were still a few empty desks, actually, but once it seemed no one else would be arriving – he got to his feet. He put his palms on the surface of the desk and leaned forward.

'All right,' he said, hoping no one heard the nervous tremor in his voice. 'Where did Professor Ullman leave off?'

A male student, thin and young – pale cheeks still smooth and free of stubble despite the fact that his hair was dark – raised his hand and, without waiting to be called upon, said, 'Conic sections'.

Simon blinked.

'Chronic what?'

Two hours later it was over.

He fell into the chair behind his desk, covered in a thin gloss of garlic-stinking sweat, his carefully combed hair now hanging in his face. He exhaled in a sigh and watched the students grab their bags and strap them over their shoulders, turn their phones back on, pull cigarettes from their pockets and pack them against the backs of their hands, and shuffle out of there for the courtyard or their next class or home or one of the fast-food joints that sur-rounded the campus.

He ran his fingers through his hair and then wiped his sweat-damp and pomade-oiled palms against the legs of his pants.

His thoughts were directed inward and he didn't even notice the girl until she was standing directly in front of him, her knees inches from his knees, her breasts directly in front of his eyes. He tilted his head up to look at her face. She was maybe eighteen, certainly no older than twenty. She was wearing a short skirt and a white blouse. Her hair was short and black. A backpack was strapped over her right shoulder, and there were childish tchotchkes – lanyards and key-chain ornaments – hanging from the various zippers. But there was also something sensuous about her that – combined with the childishness still cling-ing to her despite her tentative steps toward adulthood – made Simon uncomfortable. A woman's body despite the young face and something in the eye that said she knew a lot more than she pretended. Or perhaps she was pretend-ing to know more than she did.

'I was worried about you, Professor,' she said. 'Where did you get that scar on your cheek?'

'I cut myself shaving.'

'It's kind of sexy.'

'And you are?'

'Is this some kind of game?'

Simon smiled out of nervousness, because he didn't know what else to do.

She smiled back.

'Kate Wilhelm,' she said, and Simon saw by the sparkle in her eye that she thought it was indeed a game of some sort. 'And I'm having an awfully difficult time learning all the hard, hard math you teach.' She sat on his lap. Simon saw something like nervousness flicker behind the eyes and realized that she was acting, playing a part she'd seen in movies, or imagined herself playing while sprawled out on her bed, pretending to be all grown up. He could understand that: playing a role you had been assigned or had assigned yourself. It was part of life, wasn't it? Every day, in order to live with others, you pretended to be something just a little different from what you really were. That it was obvious with Kate, that the role she was playing didn't quite fit on her, made him like her. 'Maybe you can tutor me. I saw in the paper that your wife has a thing tonight. Maybe I can come over and we can run through some equations.'

'She expects me,' he said. 'Tonight. To be there.'

'So,' Kate said. 'Go but leave early. She has to stay all night. You don't.' She stood up and touched the scar on his face, ran a red-painted fingernail along it. 'I'll be waiting for you.'

'I'll think about it,' he said.

'Oh, goody.'

She stood and pivoted on a shiny black shoe and

swayed away, sparing a glance and a 'See you later' before she disappeared into the hallway.

Simon tongued the inside of his mouth and felt a heaviness in his gut like he'd swallowed a brick.

He ate lunch – which is to say he ordered lunch and picked at it without eating much of anything – at a Greek sandwich joint on Ventura in North Hollywood. Once he'd tired of staring at the food on his plate – a gyro and hummus and tabouleh – he got back into his car. He took Ventura to Lankershim, and drove north toward Dr Zurasky's office.

Ten minutes later he pulled into a parking lot in front of a strip mall. The first floor was filled with standard businesses – a pizza joint and a dry cleaner's and a barber shop and a liquor store – but the second floor had quiet little businesses with no signs, or small signs that couldn't be read until you were already upstairs. The kind of places you'd never see unless you already knew they were there.

Dr Zurasky's office was on the second floor between an aromatherapy place and a medical marijuana place.

He pulled open the fingerprinted glass door and walked into the cool blue reception room.

Ashley was sitting behind her desk, and when he walked in she glanced up. At first, there was a look of confusion on her face, and then she smiled.

'Hello, Mr Shackleford.'

'Ashley.'

'How are you today?'

'I've been worse.'

'That's thinking positive. I'll let Dr Zurasky know you're here.'

She got to her feet and walked around her desk. She did not have a pretty face – she was rather plain and her hair was dull and flat and colorless – but she had unbelievable legs, long and muscular and perfectly shaped, and Simon was pretty sure she knew it. She took every opportunity to show them off. She could as easily have let Zurasky know Simon was here by telling him over the phone's intercom. She poked her head into Zurasky's office and said something inaudible, pulled her head out, and closed the door.

'He's got a few more minutes with his one o'clock.'

Simon nodded and sat down on a vinyl couch.

There were several magazines spread across a coffee table, but he didn't even consider picking one up. Instead, he sat there wondering where Zurasky fit into the picture. He had something to do with this. Simon couldn't figure out what though. He had been Shackleford's doctor as well. It couldn't be simple coincidence that two men who were nearly identical had been seeing the same shrink. Never mind the fact that Simon hadn't seen him in over a year. Los Angeles probably had more shrinks per capita than any other city in the world – it certainly had more people who needed one – so it couldn't be simple coincidence. Somehow Zurasky was involved.

That thought made Simon feel sick to his stomach. Had Zurasky been manipulating Shackleford? Had he been—

'Hey, Jeremy.'

Simon looked up. Zurasky was standing in the doorway to his office and the glass front door was swinging shut behind a heavyset blonde woman who was wearing a pair of pink sweatpants and a man-sized T-shirt.

'Hi.'

Zurasky was a kind-looking man with a wild head of hair and round cheeks and glasses. He was wearing a pair of striped slacks and a blue shirt with one of the sleeves rolled up and a pink tie with pictures of golfers on it. He had one bad arm, a stump which he said he was born with. It grew about six inches past the elbow and ended in a smooth rounded-off mound, but today the sleeve was folded over it and pinned up so it wouldn't flap about like a windsock.

He smiled a wide open smile.

'Are you coming in?'

Simon blinked.

Zurasky suddenly seemed cold behind the jolly facade.

Simon stood up, took a step toward Zurasky, and then stopped.

'You know – I've changed my mind.'

'You're already here,' Zurasky said. 'You can't change your mind.'

'But I have.'

'Nonsense. Come on.'

He stepped aside and gestured for Simon to enter his office. Simon had seen it many times – blue walls and carpet, just like the waiting room, with a big oak desk and shelves lined with books and a vinyl chair and couch that matched the one he'd just been sitting on – but somehow today it seemed incredibly uninviting. He didn't want to go in there. He didn't want to go in there at all – not until he knew how Zurasky fit into this.

Simon shook his head and backed toward the glass door.

Ashley simply sat at her desk. The phone was to her ear but she was staring at Simon. He didn't like the look on her face. She was probably in on it – whatever it was.

'Jeremy,' Zurasky said. There was a sternness in his voice, but he kept on smiling. Simon didn't like it. His adoptive father, when leaving a car dealership, or flipping the channel on a politician or a televangelist, had liked to repeat a saying he attributed (incorrectly, Simon thought) to Mark Twain: 'Never trust a man who prays in public or one who smiles all the time.' While he hadn't liked his adoptive father much, it had always seemed very good advice.

Simon shook his head again, turned around, and pushed his way out the door.

*

If he'd considered what Samantha had said this morning – that Jeremy Shackleford had been seeing Dr Zurasky – he would have realized sooner that he was somehow involved in the break-in, even if indirectly. He had to be. It couldn't be a simple coincidence. But he hadn't thought about it. His mind had been focused on making sure Samantha believed him to be her husband.

But now, knowing that Zurasky was somehow in-volved, Simon felt an intense urge to get the corpse out of his bathtub – what was left of the corpse. When he thought no one knew – no one but Robert, who seemed to have kept his promise – holding on to the body seemed the safest course of action, but if Zurasky knew, well, there was no telling what he would do.

It was time to get rid of it.

Simon parked on Wilshire, waited for a patch of traffic to pass, pushed open his door, and stepped out into the midday sunshine.

He felt cold despite the heat. He didn't know why, but he did. The sun warmed his skin but he felt cold inside.

He stepped up onto the sidewalk and headed for the Filboyd Apartments. But then he froze. Helmut Müller was walking by on the sidewalk in front of him, wearing his yellow cardigan sweater and threadbare slacks, aged skin hanging loose from his bones. He looked skeletal but he was very much alive.

He turned toward Simon as he passed him.

'Walk the mile,' he said.

'What?'

But Müller simply turned away, looked straight ahead, and walked past.

'What did you say?'

The man did not respond.

Simon grabbed him by the arm and spun him around.

'What did you say?'

Müller put his arms out to keep his balance, looking for a long moment like he might topple anyway, swaying left on one foot while his arms waved, and then finally he managed to stabilize himself. He looked up at Simon with fear in his eyes.

'I have no money.'

'I don't want money. I wanna know what you said.'

'I – I said nothing.'

'I heard you.'

The old man's eyes were wide and pale and water was building up on the bottom lids.

'I said nothing. I swear to you, sir. Please – do not – please.'

Simon grabbed his collar and shook him.

'Just tell me what you said!'

As Simon shook Müller water fell from the edges of the man's eyelids and rolled down his cheeks, flowing along the deep lines that were carved into his flesh, and a sob escaped his mouth.

'Please.'

Simon stopped.

Several people on the sidewalk were looking at him. The old man's entire body was shaking violently.

'I'm – I'm sorry.' He let go of the man's shirt.

It couldn't have been him. He was dead. It had been in the newspaper.

Walk the mile.

Did he know that Simon was wearing another man's shoes?

He couldn't know anything; he was dead.

Goddamn it – what was happening?

He pushed through the glass doors and into the lobby of the Filboyd Apartments. It smelled stale and dusty after the bright sunshine of mid-afternoon. He entered the darkened stairwell and made his way up its creaky steps.

He was three steps from the top (and seventeen steps from the bottom: he still counted every time), the light from the second-floor corridor just penetrating this far down, when he saw it on the wall. It was right where he had seen the other graffito, and he thought it had been sprayed on by the same person. The letters were formed the same way, with the same looping strokes.

WALK THE MILE

Simon stood motionless, looking at it for a long moment. His tongue felt like a dead piece of meat, dry and coarse, and it stuck to the roof of his mouth.

There was no evidence that any other writing had ever been there. The other graffito was not painted over – it just wasn't there.

Walk the mile.

He turned around and pounded back down the stairs, through the lobby, and out into the sunshine.

Cars passed by.

An old couple holding hands.

A helicopter throbbed overhead.

He glanced left, saw a homeless man sleeping on the bench in front of Captain Bligh's. He glanced right and saw a yellow cardigan disappearing around a corner.

'Hey!' he shouted.

But Müller was gone, swallowed by the edge of a building.

Simon ran down the sidewalk after him. His throat still hurt when he breathed hard. It was strange that his cheek had healed but his throat still hurt. The bruising hadn't been that bad.

He turned the corner.

Müller was gone. The side street was empty of human life. A block north traffic flowed. Then, from an alley, a dog came trotting out onto the sidewalk with something in its mouth, perhaps a half-eaten hamburger.

Simon recognized the dog – he recognized it by its steak-fat ear and its one white eye with its bulging vein.

He pushed his apartment's front door closed behind him. Then he stood with his forehead pressed against the cool wood, his moist, sweaty skin sticking to the paint. His head throbbed above his left eyebrow. His eye watered.

Calm down, he told himself.

There's an explanation for this.

He pushed himself off the door and turned around.

You're okay. You're better than okay. You're on the verge of a new life. You just need to get rid of the evidence and walk away from here. If there's no evidence, then it doesn't matter what Zurasky knows or how he's involved; he won't be able to prove anything.

Forget Helmut Müller for now, forget the dog. You can find out what that's about later.

Just get rid of the evidence.

He walked into the kitchen. He found the box of trash bags underneath the sink – the cardboard slightly damp from leaking pipes – but couldn't find the other item he needed. He dug through several drawers, coming across dead batteries, broken screwdrivers, dirt-black pennies, rusty screws, bent nails, twisted spoons, and then, finally, in the last drawer in the kitchen, bottom right, hello, he found the electric carving knife and a brown extension cord he thought would probably be long enough. He had bought the carving knife while drunk at one o'clock in the morning about two months ago after watching an infomercial about it and deciding that he had to have it – though he didn't know why. Well, now he did know. He thought it would be perfect for cutting whatever meat was left between the bones, whatever was holding them together at the joints.

With the knife in one hand and the damp box of trash bags in the other he made his way down the hallway, past his bedroom, and into the bathroom.

He put the items on the tile floor, unzipped his pants, and took a leak.

He exhaled.

'I guess it's time,' he said, 'for us to part ways, Jeremy.'

He finished urinating, the last coming out as a shiver elevatored up his spine, then shook, tucked, zipped, and flushed.

'It's safer this way,' he said. 'And anyways, it had to be done sooner or later.'

He turned to the bathtub. It was empty. Someone had taken the body.

'Oh – oh, fuck.'

He walked to the bathtub and looked down into it. There was dirt lining the bottom of the tub and a brown ring running around the inside and black mold growing in the corners where it met the tiled walls, but it was empty.

He ran his fingers through his hair. It was oily and slick with pomade and sweat. The pain above his left eyebrow burrowed deeper into his brain. He wiped his palms off on his trousers. He thought he might start crying.

This was not good. This was not good at all. Who would have done this? Who would have taken the body from his tub? It had to be Zurasky, didn't it? It couldn't be anybody but Zurasky. He was the only one who had known – *if* he had known. But Simon wasn't certain he had. He was involved somehow, but he might not know everything.

Simon walked in a counter-clockwise circle, mind racing.

'Oh, God,' he said.

He looked around frantically. There was nothing to do in here. Nothing useful.

He shook his fists, looking for something to grab, to throw, to break, and when he saw nothing and the pressure in his gut which demanded action of some kind was too much to deny any longer he simply swung loose, throwing punches, one two three four, goddamn it, into the wall. It was an old building and the walls were lath and plaster, so he didn't break through. He dented the plaster and managed to crack the rotting wood beneath – dark and moist – and bruise his knuckles, but not much else.

He'd been Jeremy for less than twelve hours and already it was unraveling.

It wasn't fair.

They had bought it. They had fucking bought it. Samantha, Professor Ullman, his students, they had all bought it, but it was unraveling anyway.

Walk the mile.

He didn't have a choice now, did he?

He'd set his course the moment he decided to step into Shackleford's life. And someone knew. Someone knew and had taken the body before he could take care of it, before he could destroy all the evidence.

No – wrong. He'd had time to get rid of the body, but instead had kept it, afraid of doing what he'd known had to be done. Afraid that if he ditched the body somebody would find it. Well, someone had found it anyway. What had they done with it?

And who else besides Zurasky might know?

He sat down on the toilet and tried to think. It was difficult to do with a heavy dread in his gut, with panic on the verge of completely taking over his mind and doing with him what it wished.

Someone had taken the body.

Calm down. Think.

What next?

He had to do something to this situation before it did something to him. He had to calm down and think clearly. If he could only think clearly he'd be able to make a decision and then act upon it.

What next?

And then he knew.

'Robert,' he said aloud to the empty room.

He sat in the Saab, watching the building's entrance in his side-view mirror. It was about time for Robert's late-afternoon smoke break. Despite the fact that he could see dozens of cars driving along the streets and dozens of people walking along the sidewalks, he felt like he was in a completely different place. The car deadened the noise of the outside world and made him feel apart from it.

A homeless man walked to the window and knocked. Simon shook his head. The guy knocked again. Simon rolled down the window.

'Get out of here.'

The homeless man – forty, maybe, with a thick beard and no teeth – said, 'You gonna get out? You want some time on the meter?'

'No.'

'No you're not gonna get out or no you don't want no time on the meter?'

'Just go.'

'I'll give you some time, anyhow,' the homeless man said. He walked to the meter behind which Simon was parked, pulled out what looked like a bent paperclip, slipped it into the coin slot, jerked it up and down several times, each flip of the wrist adding fifteen minutes to the meter, stopping when the meter was at its max of two hours.

'See?' the homeless guy said. 'Gimme a buck and it's still half the price.'

'I'm not getting out of the car.'

'Come on, man, it's just a buck.'

Simon gave the guy a dollar to get rid of him.

'Now leave me alone.'

He reached into his pocket for his cigarettes, stuck one between his lips, and lighted it.

'Are those Camels? Think I could get one? I love—'

Simon threw the pack of cigarettes at the guy. It hit him in the chest and then dropped to the sidewalk.

'Get the fuck *out* of here.'

'Thanks,' the guy said, picking up the cigarettes. 'Got a ligh— Never mind. Thanks.'

He held the cigarettes up close to his ear, like a kid with a seashell, and gave the pack a shake to see how many were inside.

Simon took a drag off his cigarette and glanced in the side-view mirror toward the building's entrance. But it wasn't Robert's reflection he saw. It was the actual man. He had already moved past the side of the car and was walking onward. He must have been out of cigarettes himself, walking to that liquor store on Fourth Street to grab a pack.

Simon pushed open the door and stepped out and slammed it shut behind him. He followed Robert down the sidewalk, and when Robert walked past an alleyway

Simon rushed him, shoved him into the stinking gray air of that narrow slice between two buildings, and slammed the man against a rusted green dumpster.

'Was it you?' he said as the burning cigarette bounced around in his mouth.

'Wha—'

'Were you the one who took it?'

'Took what?'

'You know what, goddamn you,' Simon said, shaking Robert, slamming him against the dumpster a second time. 'Did you take it or not?'

'I don't know what you're talk—'

Simon grabbed him by the shirt collar and threw him left, slamming him against a red brick wall. Then he grabbed the shirt collar again and put his face inches from Robert's face, the cherry of the cigarette in his mouth floating a mere jostle from Robert's waiting flesh.

'Don't you fucking lie to me.'

'I don't.'

'You don't what?'

'Know what you're talking about.'

'Oh, bullshit!'

Robert fumbled for the inside pocket of his thin suit coat. 'I have money.'

'Do I look like I want your money?'

'I don't know what—'

'Just answer the fucking question.'

'I didn't, okay? I didn't fucking take it.'

Simon let go of the man and he crumpled to the dirty ground amongst a litter of paper cups, rotting food, and other refuse.

Robert wasn't lying. One thing Simon knew was that Robert was incapable of lying convincingly. He didn't know what Simon was talking about despite the suspect circumstances under which he had visited Simon's apartment. Maybe he really had simply dropped his cell phone into the toilet. Maybe his visit had been exactly what it appeared to be. It didn't make sense to Simon – he was the only person Simon knew had seen the body, who Simon was sure knew about it – but a lot of things didn't make sense today.

He turned away and headed back out of the alley, taking another drag from his cigarette. It tasted bad, but he smoked it anyway.

'Fuck,' he said.

Maybe Robert had improved as a liar. Either way, he wasn't going to get anything out of the man himself. Coming here had been dumb, a panic move. Had he expected Robert just to crumble? 'Okay, you caught me. I took the body. I thought I could use it for the carpool lane.'

As he walked back toward the Saab he decided to go to Robert's apartment and see what he came up with. Maybe he had the body there – or something that would help him figure out who did have it and why they took it. Any information would be better than what he had now.

*

After driving toward the ocean for several miles Simon turned right onto Western and took it toward Hollywood. Bent palms jutted upwards, drooping above the houses and businesses like wind-frayed umbrellas. By the time he reached Lexington he could make out the Hollywood sign through the mist, perched crookedly on its hillside.

It didn't rain much in Los Angeles, but he liked it when it did. The downpour cleared the sky and made it so you could see for miles in every direction. It washed the filth away. The town was due for a good cleansing.

A block or two shy of Sunset Boulevard Simon made a left and drove till he came to Robert's pink stucco apartment building. The narrow strip of grass in front of it – what some might call a lawn – was dead and brown. A pile of dog shit sat on it near the sidewalk, buzzing with flies.

Simon stepped from the Saab and walked toward the building, and then up onto Robert's front porch. He checked under the welcome mat and under a dead potted plant. He found a key in neither of those locations. He looked around, trying to figure out where Robert might hide a spare. He didn't want to have to break into the place – though he would. He reached up above the door and brushed his fingers across the top of the door frame. Dust fell down into his face and he shook his head and blew out through his nostrils. His fingers bumped something and it dropped to the concrete porch, tinkling like a bell. He sneezed from the dust, wiped at his nose, then wiped the results off on his pants.

The key lay at his feet. He picked it up, unlocked the front door, and went inside.

The apartment smelled of stale beer, marijuana, and the quiet depression of a man who never opened his windows or blinds. It was a small three-room apartment with a thirty-year-old green shag carpet, a small two-burner stove, and a fridge you could maybe squeeze a six-pack of Miller Lite and a package of bologna into if you were the kind of person who happened to like Miller Lite and bologna.

Simon searched the place.

Robert could have taken the body. He could have called work and said he would be late, gone to Simon's apartment, and taken it. He could have – but why?

That was a question for later. The question for now was did he.

After ten minutes of searching and finding nothing – nothing but a collection of pornography, a collection of comic books, a collection of stamps, and a collection of bongs all stinking of stale bong water – Simon decided the answer to that was no. Or, if he had, he hadn't brought it back to his apartment. Of course – why would he have?

Not knowing what else to do, Simon decided to call it a day.

*

But before heading back to Pasadena he stopped off at his apartment for what he thought might very well be the last time. If he could walk away from all this squalor, that would be just fine by him. He grabbed Francine and her small can of food, took them down to the car, and buckled her into the passenger's seat. The shoulder strap went right over the top of the jar, of course, but the waist strap held her in place. He wanted her safe.

He put the car into gear and headed for home.

Home?

Why not? It was his now. If he could keep it.

He parked the Saab in the driveway and killed the engine. He half-expected the police to be waiting for him inside, standing next to a weeping Samantha, and when he walked in they would all look up at him with hateful accusation in their eyes.

Handcuffs would be pulled from belts. Steps would be taken toward him. Someone would say, You're under arrest for the murder of—

He'd run but it would be no use. Of course it wouldn't. It never is.

He grabbed Francine and got out of the car.

The living room was empty – not a cop in sight.

He closed the front door behind him, twisting the

deadbolt home, and walked to the couch. He put Francine's Mason jar onto the coffee table, sprinkled some food onto the water, and sat there watching her eat.

'Jeremy?' Samantha said, walking out of the hallway.

She wore a skirt and a gray blouse with the top two buttons undone, revealing her small-breasted cleavage. She was putting earrings into the several holes in her ears.

'Where've you been?' she said. 'Dr Zurasky called and said you ran out of his office.'

'I'm – I did.'

'Are you okay?'

Simon shook his head.

'I – I'm – no.'

'Oh, baby,' Samantha said.

She walked to the couch and sat down next to him. She put her arms around him.

'What is it?'

'Everything,' Simon said. 'It's just – everything.' He exhaled through his nose. 'My head is killing me.'

'Want me to get you some Tylenol?'

'Okay.'

'Okay.'

Samantha got to her feet and disappeared into the hallway a moment. When she returned she was carrying three pills in the palm of one hand and a glass of water in the other.

Simon took the pills, closed his eyes a moment, and then opened them again.

He looked up at Samantha.

'Does the phrase "walk the mile" mean anything to you?'

Samantha shook her head.

'Should it?'

'I don't know.'

She bit her lip. 'I should call Gil and tell him we can't go.'

'To your show?'

Samantha nodded.

'No,' Simon said. 'I'm okay.'

'It can go on without me.'

'No. I want to go.'

It was true. He wanted to be Jeremy Shackleford and Jeremy Shackleford would go to his wife's art show. He would go and he would hold her hand and smile and be supportive. That's what husbands did. He had seen it in movies and it seemed to be true. It should be, even if it wasn't.

'Are you sure?'

He nodded. This was what he wanted; this was what he'd spent the last two weeks thinking about and dreaming about. He was sure.

'Okay,' she said. 'We don't have to leave for a couple of hours. Take a few minutes and relax.'

He nodded again.

Samantha turned away to finish getting ready, but then stopped.

'You got a goldfish?'

'Her name is Francine.'

Simon changed into a gray suit, which he thought would be more appropriate for the evening, which he thought was more like something Jeremy would wear to such an event. He washed his face, then dug through the closet till he found an overcoat, and then slipped into it.

'You're really gonna wear that?'

'I'm cold.'

'You look like a Griffith Park pervert.'

'I think I'm coming down with flu or something,' he said. 'I got the shivers.'

Samantha shrugged.

'Okay.'

The art show wasn't at a gallery but a restaurant in Silverlake, on Sunset Boulevard, not too far east of the Sunset Junction. The tables had been lined up in the center of the room, where several tapas – warm seasoned almonds, spiced olives, some kind of blue-veined Spanish cheese that looked like a moldy version of brie – were laid out artistically among various bunches of flowers.

A bartender – a twenty-something actor-type that Simon thought he recognized from a bit part on one of those police procedural shows; he'd played a rapist – stood behind the bar, looking bored. He was, Simon would bet, a bartender who liked flair, and tonight he was stuck pouring free glasses of mid-grade pinot into six-ounce plastic cups, just getting people lubricated enough to maybe buy a piece of art, to part with their money.

Samantha's paintings were hung around the room.

About forty or fifty people paced around, drinking their wine and looking at the paintings.

A moment after they walked into the restaurant a thin man with spiked hair, wearing a burgundy velvet jacket and black pants and a pair of suede platform shoes (he was short and wished he wasn't, Simon thought), came pouring toward them, all teeth and joints and blue blue eyes.

'Samantha!' he said as he arrived, kissing both of her cheeks.

'Hi, Gil,' Samantha said.

'Jeremy! Nice overcoat. Headed to a schoolyard later? Just kidding. Give it.'

Gil held his arms out to be hugged.

Simon hugged him uncomfortably.

'What happened to your face?'

'Dog bit me.'

'Oh.' Gil seemed lost for only a second. Then: 'Do you guys want some wine? Tapas?'

'Oh,' Samantha said, 'we'll make our way to the bar. No hurry.'

Gil spun around.

'Look everybody!' he shouted to the room. 'The lady of honor has arrived, the fabulous Samantha Kepler-Shackleford!' He swept his arms toward her.

She blushed and did a little curtsy.

Gil clapped for her and everybody followed his example, and then, when the clapping subsided, he said, 'Her beautiful paintings are all for sale, and worth every penny, I assure you. In sixty years when she's dead and famous, your grandchildren will be so glad of your present good taste.'

Several people chuckled.

'We've sold about half already,' Gil said in what Simon thought was an intentionally too-loud whisper.

He headed over to the bar.

An hour later he was on his third glass of wine. His head was throbbing. He was standing in a corner with Samantha. She'd circled the room smiling and shaking hands while he stood in the corner and drank, but the room was fully reconnoitered now, good prospects charmed, and they were together again. They watched the crowd. Gil was putting red stickers on the wall next to two more paintings – the last two – which meant they had now sold out.

'You don't look so good,' Samantha said.

'My head still.'

'Maybe you should—'

'Samantha?'

Simon looked up at the sound of the voice.

It belonged to a brunette with a boy's haircut and a woman's body. She had red lipstick smeared across her full lips making her look like she'd been punched in the mouth and liked it. She was wearing a short skirt and black stockings and a Pere Ubu T-shirt that said

L'Avant Garage:
Qu'est-ce que c'est?

'Marlene Biskind with the *East Sider*. Can I get a picture of you and your husband?'

'Of course,' Samantha said, slipping a hand through Simon's arm.

Marlene Biskind held up a Nikon camera with a lens like the barrel of Dirty Harry's gun.

Simon tried to smile but his eyes felt dull in his head.

A flash of light exploded in front of him and everything disappeared behind it. He blinked and people became out-of-focus silhouettes. Then a second flash. Then a third.

Simon dropped his wine, blinking, trying to regain his vision.

The wine splashed across Samantha's shoes and legs.

'Oh, shit.'

'I'm sorry.'

'It's all right.'

Gil came rushing over with a wad of napkins like he'd been standing in the corner just waiting for it to happen and started wiping at Samantha's legs and shoes and then the floor.

'My God,' he said. 'Some people just can't hold their liquor.' He stood up. 'You do it like this.' He made a cupping gesture with his empty right hand. 'Not like this.' He flattened his palm.

'I'm sorry.'

'I'm just kidding.'

'I'm—'

'It's a party. There's more wine.' And then he was off.

Marlene looked from Simon to Samantha.

'Should we try again?'

Samantha laughed. 'I think we'd better.'

She put her arm through Simon's again.

Another flash of light exploded.

Simon fell backwards. He hit the wall behind him and then slid down it. He didn't know what was wrong with him. Maybe just the day. Dogs and people coming back to life. Corpses disappearing. Impersonating a dead man. And now he was standing here pretending to smile while a woman from the *East Sider* snapped his photograph. It was all too much.

He looked up and saw Samantha and Marlene looking down at him, both with concern in their eyes. They looked incredibly tall.

'Are you okay?' Marlene said.

'Baby?'

Simon worked his way to his feet with Samantha's help.

'I'm okay. Just a little tired. It's been a long day.'

Several people had stopped their conversations and were looking at him – wine glasses or toast smeared with cheese paused halfway to or from their mouths, sentences half caught in their throats. It was obvious by the disapproving but amused looks on their faces that they thought he was drunk. He was not. He was trying to get drunk, but he felt sober as a newborn.

'We should go,' Samantha said.

'Are you sure you're okay?' Marlene said. 'You really took a spill.'

'You stay for the rest of your night, honey. This is a big deal for you. Enjoy it. I'll take a cab home.'

'Are you sure?'

Simon nodded.

'Yeah,' he said. 'I'm sure.'

The ride home took thirty minutes – thirty minutes in a blue and yellow cab that smelled vaguely of vomit and ammonia. It did nothing to improve his mental state.

He sat in the back with the window cracked.

The cab driver was not one of those guys who felt the need to fill silence with the sound of his own voice, and Simon was grateful for that at least. He just sat silently in the front seat and drove while Simon sat in the back, watching the cost of the cab ride go from its two-dollar beginnings to its thirty-six-dollar total.

The car pulled to a stop in front of Simon's – it's mine now, goddamn it – front yard. The house was silent and dark but for a lamp in the living room whose light was shining yellow through a crack in orange striped curtains. Simon gave the cab driver two twenties – keep the change; hey, thanks, buddy – and stepped from the vehicle.

He was halfway up the concrete path that bisected the lawn, watching his feet move one in front of the other, when he saw her. She had been sitting on one of the steps that led up to the front door, and as he approached she got to her feet.

'I thought you'd never get here.'

She wrapped her arms around his neck.

He had forgotten all about Kate Wilhelm.

'Hi,' he said.

He shut the door behind him and put his back against it. Kate stood only a couple of feet away. He could smell soap on her skin and lotion and perfume. Her eyes had been painted black, her lips red.

She dragged a finger across the scar on his face.

'It really is sexy,' she said.

'Thank – thank you.'

Kate laughed.

'You seem a little tense.'

She stepped to him until he could feel her breath on his neck, warm and wet.

She ran her hand down his chest. It made his skin tingle. This felt like a dream. The entire day did – it felt unreal and wrong and like a dream. But he knew it wasn't.

Kate ran the flat of her palm over the front of Simon's pants. He heard a small gasp escape his own throat and felt his heartbeat thumping in his chest.

'Oh,' she said. 'You seem really tense down here.'

Simon shoved Kate's skirt up around her waist and pulled down her panties, hearing them tear as he did. There was nothing intimate about what followed. He pushed her down on the bed, licked his fingers and rubbed them over her mound, which was smooth and recently waxed or shaved. The scent was strong and erotic. He grabbed his penis at the base and put himself inside her. She spasmed tight around him. He thrust as deep as he could, getting out everything he had in him, getting out all the frustration and fear and turmoil he was feeling inside. He ran the palms of his hands over her breasts, unbuttoned her blouse and reached inside. Her nipples were hard and she groaned. He pinched them. She reached up and scratched at his chest. He put a thumb into her mouth and she sucked on it. She grabbed his hips and pulled him even deeper into her, again and again and again.

In three minutes it was over.

Afterwards Simon put his pants back on. He felt guilty about what had happened. He felt guilty about everything. A constant cloud of guilt hung over him.

He sat on the couch, Kate beside him, and played with his Zippo lighter, lighting it and snuffing the flame repeatedly.

'How long have we known each other?'

'What?'

'How long have we known each other?' he asked again.

'Since last spring.'

Simon nodded.

'What's bothering you?' Kate asked.

'My conscience.'

Kate smiled, licked her lips.

'Simon,' she said, 'nobody has a clear conscience – except maybe sociopaths. Everybody's done something they'd rather not have done.'

He nodded. But then he found himself very bothered by what she had just said. For a long moment he couldn't figure out what it was. He replayed the sentence in his head and examined each word – something wasn't right about what she had said – and then, after a minute, he knew.

'Why did you just call me Simon?'

'I didn't.' She got to her feet. 'Anyway, I should get out of here before your wife comes home. That's a kind of awkwardness I'd rather not experience.'

She looked down at herself, smoothed the wrinkles out of her skirt, and headed for the door.

Before she reached it – her arm outstretched, extended toward the knob – Simon got to his feet and cut her off, blocking her path.

'You did. You called me Simon. I heard you. What do you know?'

Kate's eyes went scared.

'This isn't funny.'

'I'm not laughing. What do you know?'

'Jeremy, please.'

'Does the phrase "walk the mile" mean anything to you?'

She took a step back.

'My God, you are crazy.'

'Who said I'm crazy?'

'Just let me go.'

Simon grabbed a handful of Kate's hair and pulled her toward him.

'You're in on it, aren't you? *Aren't* you?'

Kate pried his hand away from her hair, the fear suddenly gone from her eyes, replaced by anger, and once she was free of his grip she pulled back and slapped him hard across the face.

'What the hell is the matter with you?'

Simon touched his fingers to his cheek and felt the skin rising in a welt and he felt moisture at the corner of his mouth. When he looked at his fingers he saw blood on them. He wiped the blood off onto his pants.

'Someone is trying to ruin me. I think it might be Zurasky and I think you're in on it. It's not gonna work.'

'I don't know who Zurasky is.'

'A lie.'

'Jeremy, I—'

'It's not gonna work.'

'I think it is working, Jeremy. You're acting crazy. You're not acting like yourself at all.'

'What is that supposed to mean?'

'What?'

'I'm not acting like myself. First you call me by another name and then you suggest – what?'

'I don't know—'

'What is this?'

'What is what?'

'Who's doing this to me?'

'Would you please just let me go? I don't – I don't—'

The fear had returned. Tears were welling in her eyes. It was Simon's day for making people's eyes well with tears.

'You don't *what*?'

'I just want to go. You need help and I don't know what to do and I just want to go.'

'You called me Simon.' But as time passed he was becoming less and less sure of that. Perhaps he had misheard. Hadn't he thought for a moment that Professor Ullman had threatened to rip out his heart? Hadn't he misheard that? He thought so – unless Professor Ullman was in on it too.

'I didn't, Jeremy. I don't even know anyone *named* Simon. Can I please just go?'

He licked his lips, wiped at the corners of his mouth. After a moment he stepped aside.

He followed her outside, and as she walked across the street to her yellow 1967 Chevy Nova he padded barefoot down the steps and watched her. His hands were in his pockets. The night air was cool and the thin sliver of the crescent moon hung like a fish-hook in the sky. Simon wondered what God was fishing for. If there was a God.

If God existed, and if He paid any attention, He was surely laughing at those who would drop to their knees and pray for the sick and the injured and the poor whom He had sickened and hurt and dropped into squalor to begin with. Laughing and dangling that fish-hook moon, making sure He caught anyone who thought they might escape and throwing them back down to Earth to face what they had coming.

Maybe Jesus had gotten away, floated into the heavens, but nobody else would. And Simon suspected Jesus's ascent was just a story that people told themselves anyway, a story passed down through the generations that made it possible for people to live with the world they saw around them: at least escape was possible. But Simon knew something about spheres. And even if you managed to get off this planet, even if you found a way to get up and away from this low life, to float toward the heavens, there was that fish-hook moon there to catch you before you'd made a full escape.

He tongued the inside of his mouth, plucked one of the hairs out, and watched Kate get into her car.

The engine sputtered to life and the headlights shot yellow beams out into the street. Then the driver's side window rolled down and Kate turned to look at him.

'One thing before I go.'

'What's that?'

'You might want to ask yourself why you can't remember anything that happened during the month of May last year.'

She then put the car into gear and drove away before Simon could respond.

He stood in the bathroom. The light was off, but enough splashed in from the master bedroom for him to see clearly his reflection in the mirror. He tongued the inside of his cheek and looked at himself. He touched his cheek where Kate had slapped him. The welt had already gone down. He ran his finger down the scar on his cheek.

What was he missing? There was something big and obvious that he wasn't seeing, and if he could just make himself see it, all of this would make some kind of sense. What was he missing? He had to figure it out. This was turning him into a monster. Everywhere he looked he saw conspiracy; in every face someone conspiring against him. Every voice he heard was someone whispering about him. Every siren was a cop coming to collect him.

But that didn't make sense. Everyone couldn't be plotting against him.

Kate had mentioned last May and she was right. It was blank. How could she know that? What did she know about last May that he didn't? What had been erased from his mind? What happened last May?

It had been in April – seventeen or so months ago – that he had last seen Zurasky. Was there a connection there, a reason that after the blank month he had stopped seeing his psychiatrist? Had Zurasky done something to him in that blank space?

What was he missing?

He had only wanted to know why Shackleford broke into his apartment, why Shackleford had wanted him dead, and instead he was tangled up in something that grew more and more confusing. He felt like a man trying to untie a knot whose every movement only tangled things further.

What was he missing?

Goddamn it – what the fuck was he missing?

'Figure it out, you stupid fuck!'

He punched his reflection and glass shattered around him, breaking him into hundreds of sharp pieces. Shards fell into the basin and onto the tile floor. The noise of the glass falling was incredibly loud in his ears – and then it was over and there was only silence.

3

SURFACING

He lay in bed looking up at the ceiling. It was smooth and white. The only light in the room came in through the window from the fish-hook moon.

His right hand stung and blood oozed from a network of slices in his flesh like veins of color in a marble surface. It poured onto the white comforter and spread there, blooming like a flower, as the fabric absorbed it.

Then a sound came from the living room, the sound of a key sliding into a lock, a lock tumbling, a door opening. A brief cool breeze blew through the house. The door was closed, the deadbolt twisted, the breeze stilled. Simon listened, waiting to hear who it was. He thought he knew. He was waiting for their call: It's the police. We have a warrant for the arrest of—

'Jeremy?'

It was Samantha. Of course. The police wouldn't have

a key. Her footsteps thudded across the hardwood floor, nearing him and growing louder.

The door was pushed open, squeaked open, brushed across the carpet, making a sound like leaves in a breeze, and a silhouette stood in the doorway, like a backlit gunman in an old Western movie who's just shoved through the batwings.

'Jeremy?'

'I'm in bed.'

Simon sat up, putting his back against the headboard.

'Do you mind if I turn on the light?'

'Go ahead. How was the rest of the night?'

'It was good. Too much talking. That Marlene Biskind turned out to be very nice. We exchanged information. I think we're gonna have coffee tomorrow.'

The overhead light clicked on.

Samantha kicked off her shoes.

'It was fun,' she said, 'but I'm glad it's over. Are you feeling better?'

She looked at him for the first time since coming into the room. Her face blanched. Her mouth hung open and then snapped shut.

'Oh my God.'

'Is something the matter?'

'Your hand.'

Simon lifted his hand up in front of his eyes and looked at it. It was gloved in blood, and the blood was running down his arm, tickling the thousands of blondish hairs beneath the sleeve of his shirt, which was stained red.

'Oh,' he said. 'That.'

'What did you do?'

'I hurt myself.'

'How?'

'Broke the medicine cabinet. It was – ' he closed his eyes to think and then opened them again – 'it was confusing me.'

He sat on the edge of the bathtub. He was wearing slacks and a white shirt. His sleeves were rolled up to the elbows. Samantha sat on the bathtub beside him, carefully picking shards of mirror from his flesh. Once she got the largest pieces out, she picked the tiny slivers from his hand with tweezers, and then wiped the blood away with cotton balls.

A shiver jerked through Simon's body.

'Hold still.'

'Sorry.'

'Are you cold?'

Simon nodded. 'So your show went well?'

'I told you it did. We sold out. I wasn't expecting that at all.' She went silent and continued wiping at his hand for a moment. Finally: 'I want you to see Dr Zurasky tomorrow.'

'He's not that kind of doctor. He can't do anything for my hand.'

'It's not your hand I'm worried about.'

'I don't trust him.'

Samantha wrapped gauze around Simon's hand. The bottom layers turned red with blood as more of it oozed from beneath his flesh. She continued wrapping his hand until the gauze was thick enough that the blood didn't soak through it.

'I know that, Jeremy,' she said. 'You never trust anyone when you get like this. But you need to see him.'

She taped the gauze into place.

'I'm not going to see him. Not as a patient, anyway.'

'What does that mean?'

Simon shook his head but said nothing else.

'You need to see *someone*.'

'How can I see someone when I don't know who can be trusted?'

Samantha let go of Simon's hand. She sat staring for a moment, her eyes glazed over and far away. Her chin trembled. Then her body collapsed into itself as she let go of her posture – her shoulders drooping, her chin nearly resting on her chest – and she breathed out heavily through her nostrils. Then she looked up at Simon. The emotion was gone from her eyes. Her mouth was tight. She swallowed.

'I don't know if I can keep doing this, Jeremy,' she said. 'I can't keep pretending you're still the man I married.

You've changed. I'm tired of picking up the pieces. I'm tired of *having* to pick up the pieces. I'm just – I'm fucking tired.'

After Samantha fell asleep Simon crawled out of bed and slipped back into his clothes, overcoat included. He picked it up from the back of the couch, where Kate had tossed it after pulling it off him, and put it on as he walked toward the door. He stepped out of the front door and into the night. He packed his cigarettes, slapping the packet against the back of his hand, opened it, put it to his mouth, pinched a filter between his teeth, and pulled the box away. He lighted his cigarette. He inhaled deeply and walked out to the sidewalk. The street was quiet, the world asleep all around him.

But something was wrong. Something out here had changed – in a bad way, in a way that had something to do with what was happening to him.

He closed his eyes and tried to create an image of what the street had looked like earlier, when he had left for the college this morning. He laid that image over what the street looked like right now, like a transparency, trying to see the difference. Something had been added or removed. Something had changed.

After a moment he knew. His Volvo was gone.

When he first arrived this morning he'd parked his

Volvo on the street about six houses down, but now someone's yellow Mustang was parked there.

Someone had taken it. Someone was manipulating things. Someone who could be in many places simultaneously, or coordinate several people.

He took a deep drag from his cigarette and exhaled through his nostrils.

He needed to walk, to think about this, to figure out what to do next. He started down the sidewalk, heading toward Colorado. He had no destination in mind. He just needed to move, to get blood flowing through his brain so he could think. He felt dull and stupid. He felt scared.

An engine roared to life, a pair of headlight beams splashed across his back. He froze a moment, considered glancing over his shoulder, but changed his mind. He would just keep walking, pretending he wasn't bothered, and see what the car did. It was probably nothing, just some guy who worked nights. As he walked the car rolled along behind him. It didn't gain speed and take off down the street. It simply followed.

Unable to resist any longer Simon glanced over his shoulder. A Cadillac – big and rectangular and funereal – was rolling along behind him. He thought it was black, but color was a strange thing beneath the light of the moon, and because of the headlights shining in his eyes he could not see who was driving.

He continued walking. No matter how much he tried to resist the urge to increase his speed, he found himself moving faster and faster. By the time he reached Colorado he was running, and still the Cadillac was behind him, following him.

He ran along Colorado, glancing behind him again and again as he did, feeling cool night air stinging his throat. The Cadillac was still there. It was in the right lane, simply following him, other cars swerving around it. He ran through the night from shadow to light, shadow to light, through the spotlights of the street lamps on the boulevard. A stitch sewed itself into his side. His legs started to feel rubbery and weak. Closed businesses sat dark on either side of him.

He turned down a side street and kept running. The car turned behind him and continued to follow.

A train was nearby. The sound of metal wheels rolling along metal tracks, the wind that the train's motion was creating, the screech of the train braking.

He looked around, saw steps leading down to the Memorial Park train platform. He saw the light rail train stop and the doors open. It was only three cars long, as almost no one was using the metro at this late hour. A few people got on and a few people got off.

He leaped down the stairs, in two long strides, and ran for the train.

The doors closed when he was still ten feet away.

He pounded the button and the doors opened.

He looked over his shoulder and saw a shadowy figure

in sunglasses and a black suit coming down the stairs toward the train, black tie flapping over the left shoulder.

He stepped on. The doors closed. The figure was still outside.

The train started moving, rolling along the tracks.

The figure stood on the platform outside and watched him as the train rolled away.

He rode the train – past Highland Park and Chinatown – to the end of the line. All the doors opened. A voice over a loudspeaker said everyone had to get off. The train was now out of service. He stepped onto a platform. Amtrak and Metro-Link trains were stopped at other platforms. People were standing and sitting with luggage piled beside them.

For a moment Simon considered getting on one of those trains, a train that led out of town, away from all of this. It was a great urge, but he suspected that whatever this was, whatever was going on, it couldn't be remedied geographically. Walk the mile: he had to see this to the end, whatever it was.

He took the stairs down into Union Station.

It was nearly empty inside. A janitor was pushing a dust mop back and forth across the red and black concrete. His face was skeletal, cheekbones large and jutting, hollows in his cheeks like he was sucking them in, eyes like two black holes, mouth droopy on the left side and a little bit of drool hanging there.

Simon knew he was being paranoid, but he couldn't help but feel that the man was watching him as he walked by. He didn't turn his head as Simon passed, but his eyes seemed to follow him.

After looking at a map of the various train routes, Simon made his way down two sets of escalators to the subway, walking beneath a concrete ceiling that looked like it was dripping sewage through several cracks, brownish-yellow stalactites clinging on up there as liquid ran down them and splashed to the ground beneath. Orange cones blocked off the corridor beneath the worst of the drippage. The Red Line would take him to within a quarter mile of the Filboyd Apartments. Then he could walk the rest of the way.

He didn't know where else to go.

Whoever was following him knew where Shackleford lived, but he might not know where Simon's apartment was. He might, of course – but he might not. And he needed to get a grip on what was happening here, to wrap his mind around it.

The Volvo was parked on the street in front of the Filboyd Apartments. It was empty and dark, the doors locked. It just sat there being a car and Simon stood looking at it as if he expected it to do otherwise.

'Well, take him.'

He spun around. The sidewalk was empty. He was sure, though, that he'd heard Helmut Müller's thin voice. It still echoed in his mind.

He pushed his way through the front doors and walked up the narrow flight of stairs toward his apartment. As he walked up he saw someone's back, and then a pair of legs and feet at the top of the stairs. The shoes were old suede, slick with age. The sport coat the man was wearing was brown corduroy with leather elbow patches. The hair was gray. He was spray-painting something onto the wall opposite the stairs. There was a hissing sound coming from his direction.

'Hey!'

Simon ran up the last several steps.

The man in the corduroy coat finished painting quickly and darted left, out of Simon's sight.

When he reached the top of the stairs he turned left and looked down the corridor. A brown blur vanished around the corner. Simon ran after it, past his apartment, down the leopard-spotted carpet. He could smell roasting beef coming from an apartment that opened into the corridor. He turned left again, not knowing what was just around the corner.

As soon as he did, something hit him on the forehead – two fists clenched together and brought down like a hammer – knocking him to the ground. The floor rushed up and hit him in the backside. The ceiling spun. He heard an involuntary grunt escape him, pushed out by the fall.

And then he was being trampled on. He turned over onto his belly, got onto his hands and knees, and then pushed himself up onto his feet. He looked back down the corridor, in the direction from which he'd just run. It was empty.

He thought he could hear the man thudding down steps.

His heart was pounding in his chest. He walked back through the corridor and looked into the dark stairwell.

Halfway down lay a lump on one of the steps. The stairwell was so dark, he couldn't tell what it was. He walked down and picked it up. It was a shoe. He recognized it, the old suede, the broken and tied-together shoelaces. He'd left these shoes back in Pasadena this morning, along with his car and the corduroy coat the man had been wearing. He carried the shoe back upstairs.

On the wall opposite the stairwell, on a patch of fresh white paint (Leonard must have just had it done earlier today), the graffito said

WELL, TAKE HIM

Simon touched the paint and looked at his finger. It was black, like he'd just been booked down at the police station. He wiped it off on the wall, smearing an 's' above the lettering.

He stared at it for a long time.

He was inside his apartment and twisting the deadbolt home before he realized that the door had been repaired. He unlocked the door, opened it, looked out into the empty corridor, then closed it and listened to it latch. He locked it again. He slid the chain into place. Had it still been broken when he came back earlier to get Francine? He couldn't remember. He remembered taking out his keys and unlocking the door. He remembered that. But he couldn't remember whether he'd stuck a key into the doorknob or a padlock. Could Leonard have had it done today while someone was here painting the corridor wall? It was possible, he supposed, but then wouldn't there be screw holes in the wood of the door? Certainly Leonard wouldn't have replaced—

He turned his back to the door and leaned against it.

He tossed the suede shoe onto the coffee table.

Vertigo swept over him. The world tilted sideways. He grabbed onto the wall to keep himself upright. Once the feeling passed, he looked around the room.

It was empty but for him and the furniture – his old couch, his coffee table.

Someone upstairs flushed a toilet and the pipes in the walls let out a sad cry. He could hear someone's radio playing, the sounds of traffic coming into the building through the paper-thin windows; someone with a deep voice boomed laughter.

'Hello?' he said. 'Is anybody here?'

He searched the apartment and found it empty and got a bottle of whiskey from the kitchen and sat down on the couch. Tonight was no night to bother with glasses. He twisted off the top and drank directly from the bottle. It was harsh and strong and good. There was half a bottle left and he wanted to down it all but he knew he couldn't allow himself to do that. He needed his mind working. He already felt confused and afraid as it was and drinking more would only make it worse. It would make him feel better but it would make it worse in the long run. He took another swig, wiped his lips with the back of his hand, wiped at the corners of his mouth with thumb and index finger, rolled what he found there together between them, flicked it to the floor, and set the bottle down on the coffee table.

He wanted to go to sleep, but he couldn't – not here.

That man might be back, or somebody else might, and he'd be defenseless in his sleep.

He had come here to get away, but he'd gotten away from nothing. Until he worked this thing out he could stay neither here nor at the house in Pasadena. He would have to get a motel room. That man might be back at any moment.

He got to his feet and headed for the door.

His keys were gone. He had found the door unlocked or he would have noticed when he got here. At some point in the day someone must have taken them from his pocket. That explained how his car had gotten here. Whoever took his keys – the man who was wearing his clothes – had driven it here.

Kate Wilhelm was the only person who'd been close enough to take them but she hadn't done it alone. She had seduced him, gotten him separated from his keys, and someone else had taken them. While he had been with Kate in the bedroom someone had sneaked into the living room. That was where he'd left his overcoat, which had had both sets of keys as well as Jeremy's wallet stuffed into its pockets. But only one set of keys was taken – Simon's. And apparently the clothes he was wearing when he arrived in Pasadena this morning.

But what mattered was who was behind this. The man behind the curtain. The Great and Powerful Oz. Someone was organizing this; someone was trying to drive him mad. It had to be Zurasky. The doctor was the only connection between him and Jeremy, and whoever was doing this knew who he was. Robert still might be involved some-how, maybe simply as an informant, but Zurasky had to be organizing this. Simon didn't know why or how, but it had to be him. The more he thought about it, the more it seemed there was no alternative. He had been manipulating Jeremy during their sessions, must have talked Jeremy into breaking into his apartment, into trying to kill him.

Simon couldn't remember doing anything that deserved death, but he must have done something to warrant death in someone's eyes: someone had tried to kill him.

Zurasky would be home in bed at this hour. His office would be empty. His records would be there unguarded. Perhaps there was something in Shackleford's file that would prove useful, or maybe something in his own file.

He wanted sleep, but he thought he should take care of this first. If he didn't do it tonight, it would have to wait another day, and by then – well, who knew what might have happened by then?

He had no vehicle here. He was a payroll accountant and knew nothing about hot-wiring cars, which meant his Volvo was useless to him. And Los Angeles's train system didn't go within two miles of Zurasky's office. He had to take the train back to Pasadena to get the Saab, then drive that into North Hollywood. Then he would find a motel room and get the sleep he so desperately needed.

He just had to hope that the Cadillac that had been following him was no longer there. He didn't want whoever was driving it to be a witness to tonight's activities. For all Simon knew the guy worked for Zurasky. In fact, it seemed likely. Simon couldn't think of anybody else who might want him followed.

If the Cadillac was there, Simon would have to ditch it before going to Zurasky's office. He didn't want to be followed, and he didn't want to be stopped.

He stayed out of the light of the moon, sticking to shadows, as he walked through the night-quiet suburban neighborhood toward the Saab. As he slithered from shadow to shadow, he kept an eye on the street, looking for the Cadillac. He didn't see it.

He reached the Saab, used Jeremy's keys to unlock the door, and slid inside. It smelled of stale cigarettes and flop sweat.

Though he'd merely been walking, he was breathing hard. Only a little over two weeks ago he had been a man who worked eight hours and then drank himself to sleep; he'd been a man who talked to fewer than half a dozen people on any given day, and usually the same half dozen; a man whose days were so like one another that more than once he'd awakened on a Sunday – he worked Saturdays – and driven to the office only to find it closed. And been disappointed. How was he supposed to fill these hours? The days and weeks changed, but his routine did not.

And now look where he was.

He slid the key into the ignition and started the car.

The radio blared at him, screaming out loud rock music, and he quickly shut it off.

Had he left it on? No. He didn't like rock music. He only listened to acoustic blues. But still, maybe he'd been listening to—

It didn't matter. He didn't think it did. But then how could he know what mattered and what didn't any more?

Everything couldn't be significant.

Maybe there were messages for him in the rock song that was—

He closed his eyes. He breathed in and he breathed out. He opened his eyes and put the car into gear and drove toward the corner.

He was turning left onto Colorado when he saw the headlights come to life in his rear-view mirror. It was dark out, and the headlights were half a block behind him, but he thought they might belong to the same Cadillac. It looked the same beneath the light of the moon. What light the thin sliver of the crescent moon refracted anyway.

After turning onto Colorado he watched his rear-view mirror to see what the other car did. It turned left a few seconds later, staying behind him.

He had to lose it before he started toward Zurasky's place of business – if it was the car he thought it was.

A light in front of him turned red. He slowed the car

to a stop at the intersection, found his cigarettes in his inside coat pocket, and lighted one.

The other car pulled up beside him on the right. It was definitely the same Cadillac.

Simon tried to get a look at the driver without being obvious. He stole several glances from the corner of his eye. He was a short man, his head a full six inches from the roof of the car. Simon figured that made him about five and a half feet tall, three inches shorter than Simon himself. He had the build of a jockey. Simon put him at eight stone – a hundred and twelve pounds. He was pale as a snake's belly. He wore dark sunglasses despite the night. His greasy black hair hung down to his jaw, was cut straight there, and was tucked behind his ears. He looked straight ahead, not even a glance in Simon's direction.

A car horn honked. The light was green.

Simon gassed it.

At the next block Simon cut right and swerved across two lanes. He heard the Cadillac screeching to a stop behind him. He cut right again and found himself on another empty street. He pulled to the curb and shut off his lights, letting the engine idle quietly while he sat in darkness, watching the street behind him in his side-view mirror.

The Cadillac drove by. The pale face of the driver hovered behind the side window, but the Cadillac simply went past.

After another moment of silence Simon made a u-turn

and drove back out to the main street. Once he'd turned onto it, he flipped his headlights back on. All the way to the freeway he glanced around him, expecting to see the Cadillac, but it seemed that he'd successfully lost it.

The strip mall was dark and the parking lot empty. Doors were bolted. Alarms were set. Simon didn't know if Zurasky's office was wired with one. He had never looked for it and he had never seen one. Even if it was, he had thirty or forty minutes, unless a police cruiser happened to roll by or someone saw broken glass. Simon didn't know how else he might get inside; he was no lock picker. Unless he could get in through a window in the—

He got out of the car and walked around to the back alley, where several dumpsters sat. If he could get in through the back, that would save him the worry of witnesses. It looked like Zurasky's office window was half open. The question was whether he could get inside through it.

After a moment's thought, he walked over to the dumpsters. It was tough work moving one of them, as the wheels didn't roll very well and the thing was half-filled with garbage and heavy. It reeked and when he started pushing it he put his left hand into something slimy and rancid-smelling. He pulled his hand away and shook off what was either noodles or maggots – it was impossible to tell which – and then continued pushing. Once he had it against the wall beneath Zurasky's open window, he climbed atop it. The plastic lids were slippery, and because the dumpster's back was higher than the front, he felt like he would slip backwards and fall. He didn't.

Even on the dumpster, standing on tiptoe and reaching up, his fingers were nearly a foot shy of the window sill. He jumped up and punched through the screen and pulled it out. It fell on top of him, a corner of the aluminum frame crashing into the top of his head before it clattered to the asphalt below. Fortunately the screen was light. Still, he slipped and fell onto his side on the dumpster's lid.

But the window was clear. There was no sound of alarm. He'd been worried there would be some kind of motion sensor attached to the window, but apparently not – unless it was a silent alarm. He'd find out soon enough.

He got back onto his feet, jumped up, and found himself hanging from the window sill. The metal frame cut into the palms of his hands. His right hand started bleeding again and throbbing with pain. He grunted and struggled to pull himself up. It was much more difficult than it looked. He hadn't done any kind of exercise in years and his arms felt weak and thin. But he pulled with his arms and kicked with his feet, scuffing the toes of his shoes. After a few minutes, his upper body was over the ledge, and he just lay there, breathing hard, window frame cutting into his gut.

Once he'd got his breath back he climbed the rest of the way into Zurasky's office.

He examined the window and decided there was no alarm attached to it, and then he pulled the shade closed and turned on the office light, illuminating the desk and the blue walls and carpet and the vinyl chair and couch. He looked around for a file cabinet but didn't see one. He thought it was probably in the front office, but his chest hurt from the physical exertion, so he decided to sit down for a minute first. He looked through Zurasky's desk. He found a bottle of vodka in the bottom right drawer. Vodka wasn't usually his drink of choice, but it would do in a pinch. Hell, mouthwash would do in a pinch – a little spearmint wine to pass the time. He unscrewed the cap, wiped the top of the bottle off with his overcoat's sleeve, and took a swallow. He closed his eyes.

Eventually his breathing went back down to normal and his chest stopped hurting.

After another swallow of vodka he got to his feet and went out to the front office. It was strange to be in here alone. It felt unnatural. There was no file cabinet out here either. All the files must be digital. He walked to Ashley's desk and sat down and moved the mouse around. The previously silent computer began to hum as its interior fan whirled, and the dark screen came aglow.

After some clicking around he found what he thought were probably the patient files, but the folder was password-protected. He tried seven or eight passwords, guessing what

Zurasky's thought processes might be for each, and each time he was wrong. He looked through Ashley's drawer, hoping she had the password written down somewhere. He knew people often wrote their passwords down so they were handy in case they forgot them themselves. He did the same thing at work, not that it would have taken a genius to guess 1910 – 's' being the nineteenth letter in the alphabet and 'j' being the tenth. Simon Johnson. He found a yellow notepad with the single word

swordfish

written on it in red ink, and thought that might be the password, but when he tried it it got him nowhere. He was sure it was the password for something, but not what he wanted.

Half an hour later – after more failed guesses and another swig (or three) of vodka – he climbed back out of the window. The only thing he had gotten out of it was Zurasky's home address.

He pulled his car to the curb in front of Dr Zurasky's house. The windows were dark and only silence seeped through the walls.

He pushed open the car door and stepped out into the night.

Zurasky lived in a single-storey blue-stucco tract house

that looked like it'd been built in the seventies. It was shaped like a cracker box on its side, and had thin windows with vertical blinds, asphalt shingles on the sloped roof, and a flat yellow lawn with a small flowerbed butted up against the outer wall. The flowers in it were pink and purple and healthy despite the yellow lawn. The sound of traffic hummed in the distance.

He walked to the front door, raised his hand to knock, dropped it, and raised it again.

He told himself this wasn't like earlier. He would be asking the questions. This wasn't a session – this was an interrogation, and he was in control. Not Zurasky.

He knocked on the door, and then listened, ear tilted toward the house. He thought he could hear an inner door squeaking open, then the sound of footsteps padding toward him.

'Who – wha?'

'It's Jeremy Shackleford.'

'Jeremy – oh.' He was asleep still. 'Do you know what time it is?'

'No.'

'Well, it's—'

'We need to talk.'

'Don't you think this can wait till—'

'No. It can't wait.'

'How did you get my home add—'

'Open the door.'

A sigh. The sound of various locks being unlatched.

The door was pulled open and light splashed out onto the porch. Zurasky was on the other side. He wore blue pajama bottoms and a T-shirt. His hair was even wilder than it normally was. There were pillow creases embedded into the flesh of his right cheek. His eyes were red. He scratched at the end of his smoothly rounded-off stump, and stepped aside, leaving the doorway empty for Simon.

'Come on in, Jeremy. Let's talk.'

The living room was long and narrow. A white couch sat in the middle of it atop a white carpet surrounded by white walls on which abstract paintings hung. The coffee table was glass and had issues of psychiatry and science magazines sitting on it. Various wood sculptures sat in the corners – giraffes and elephants and something that might have been a monkey climbing a tree.

'How did you get my home address?'

'Does it matter?'

'I'd like to know.'

'I broke into your office.'

Zurasky nodded slowly, acting as if that surprised him not at all.

'And your hand?'

'Garbage disposal accident.'

Another slow nod.

'Do you want coffee?'

'Do you have whiskey?'

'I have whiskey. I'm not giving you any. Would you like a coffee?'

Simon nodded.

'Have a seat.' Zurasky gestured toward the white couch. 'I'll be back.'

Simon walked to the couch and sat down. The cushions were firm and uncomfortable.

From the kitchen, the sound of the microwave running, and then a ding. A minute later Zurasky came walking out of his kitchen with two cups of coffee. He was holding them both by their handles with his good hand and balancing them on the stump of his bad arm. It was the instant kind. There was a swirling scrim of half-melted crystals and milk foam on the surface of the liquid. Steam rose from the cups. Simon's cup was blue and Zurasky's was red. There was a chip on the top of Simon's, the white porcelain stained brown by coffee.

'Thank you.'

Zurasky nodded. Then he walked to a white chair and sat down. He sipped his coffee.

'What is this about, Jeremy?'

Simon looked down at the coffee mug, decided that he didn't trust it, and set it down on the glass coffee table without so much as a sip. That surface scrim didn't look right. He picked up a pen from the table and thumbed at the button, making the tip go in and out of the plastic casing. The pen advertised an anti-depressant whose name Simon doubted he could pronounce.

'Jeremy?'

Simon looked up.

'I know you're involved in this,' he said finally.

'In what?' Zurasky said. 'It's late. I'm not in the mood for mysteries.'

'In what's happening to me.'

'What is happening, Jeremy?' His voice was calm and his eyes were large and kind despite their sleepy redness.

'That's what I want you to tell me.'

'You're not giving me much to go on.'

'What's that supposed to mean?'

'How can I help you if you don't tell me what's going on?'

'Help me? You think I believe you want to help me?'

'What do you believe?'

'I believe you're part of this. What I want to know is how big a part – and why. Is Robert involved too? How long have you been planning it?'

'Who's Robert?'

'You mean he's not a part of it?'

'Part of what?'

'What's happening to me.'

'You're talking in circles, Jeremy.'

'You're the only person connected with both lives.'

'What are you talking about?'

'Simon Johnson.'

Zurasky was silent for a moment, eyes looking up at

the ceiling to his right. Finally he shook his head. 'Sorry. Doesn't ring a bell.'

'He was a patient of yours.'

'When?'

'Up till last April – or maybe May, but I think April.'

'For how long?'

'Couple of years, on and off – mostly off.'

'No. I would remember that.'

'You're lying.'

'Jeremy.'

'He called you just over two weeks ago to make an appointment, then cancelled.'

Zurasky's bottom lip stuck out, a thin layer of whitish skin coating it. He shook his head again.

Simon closed his eyes. He felt confused.

'When we have sessions,' he said, 'what do we talk about?'

'Whatever you want to talk about. You lead the conversation, Jeremy.'

'What do I usually want to talk about?'

Zurasky shrugged.

'Marriage troubles, problems at work, the accident. Speaking of which, I noticed you cut yourself again.'

He traced a finger across his own face from cheekbone to chinbone.

'Again?'

Zurasky nodded, then said, 'After the accident,' as if that explained everything.

'What accident?'

Zurasky sighed. 'You know damned well what accident, Jeremy,' he said. 'Why don't you tell me what's on your mind?'

'You tried to kill me.'

'I – *what*?' He looked genuinely shocked.

'You're playing head games with me. You're trying to confuse me. But I know you did. You sent Jeremy to kill me. What I want to know is why. I'll get it out of you one way or another, so you might as well tell me.'

'You're not making the least bit of sense.'

'My name is Simon Johnson. I live at the Filboyd Apartments on Wilshire. You know the place. A little over two weeks ago Jeremy Shackleford broke into my apartment and tried to murder me. He failed. Jeremy Shackleford was a patient of yours. So was I – once. You're the only human connection between us. What I want to know is why you did it. I want to know what you're up to. What I want, in short, is answers.'

Zurasky was silent for a very long time. His face was pale. He looked afraid. Simon thought that was a good thing. It meant he was on the right track. It meant he was getting to the good doctor.

'What's the matter? You seem a little—'

There was a knock at the door.

Simon jumped to his feet.

'Who is that?'

Zurasky set his coffee down on the table and stood up.

'Calm down, Jeremy. It's the police. I called them when I was in the kitchen. I was worried about you.'

'You son of a bitch.'

Simon looked around frantically, trying to find a way to escape. Zurasky had set him up. He probably had the body stored somewhere. Maybe it was in the trunk of his Volvo. Maybe this had all been part of it. Maybe Zurasky hadn't even wanted Jeremy to kill him. Maybe he'd planned this step by step and this was what it had all been leading to – his arrest for the murder of Jeremy Shackleford – his way of getting rid of both him and Jeremy. Hell, if it had happened the other way, then he'd be dead and Jeremy could be arrested for *his* murder. It wouldn't even matter who killed whom, as long as someone died. And Zurasky could get it done without bloodying his own hands at all – his own hand. But it was Simon who killed Jeremy, and Zurasky had put the body in the trunk of the Volvo and then tipped off the police as to where it was. That's what had happened. And now they were here and—

Zurasky reached out and put a hand on Simon's shoulder.

'Calm down, Jeremy,' he said. 'They're here to help.'

Simon jerked away from him.

'You calm down.'

He swung the pen in his fist toward the doctor, shoving several inches of it into the meat of his bad arm, right through his T-shirt's short sleeve. Zurasky let out a scream. Blood poured from the wound, into the cotton of the

T-shirt, down his arm, and dripped from the end of it. The doorknob rattled – 'Police! Open up!' – but the door was locked.

Simon turned and ran toward the back of the house.

He heard Zurasky unlatch the door lock, heard hinges squeak in the living room.

In the laundry room he found a door leading into the backyard. He swung it open and the darkness greeted him.

He ran out into the night, leaping over a fence and into the next yard.

Half an hour later the police had left. As had Zurasky – in an ambulance. Simon had watched from a distance and no one had even glanced at the Saab. He got lucky there.

He made his way to it and got inside. He started the engine and drove away. It was three o'clock in the morning and he was exhausted. He needed to find a place to sleep.

He took the 101 south and got off the freeway in Hollywood. He figured if he drove around he could find a dive that would take cash and wouldn't ask too many questions. He stopped at three seedy joints before he was proved correct. It seemed in this day and age even gray-market businesses expected some form of ID and a card with the Visa logo.

At first the guy behind the counter, a jowly fellow who looked like he might have insects living in his hair, wanted to charge him for thirty minutes and to see the girl Simon was bringing in – he must have just had that whore-monger look – but eventually he convinced the guy that he wanted a room for sleeping purposes only.

The guy scratched a fat face beneath a gray beard, looked at what he'd managed to scrape off with a finger-nail, flicked it away, and said, 'Suit yourself. It'll be a hundred and forty,' and slapped a key onto the stained yellow counter. 'One thirteen's around the corner, third door on the left.'

Simon thanked the guy, grabbed the key from the counter, and went to find room 113.

It stunk of misery. The threadbare yellow curtains seemed to be dripping with it. Rape and abuse and a thousand different sadnesses permeated the walls.

Simon closed the door behind him, locked it, and walked to the bed. He didn't bother undressing. He simply laid himself down on top of the covers and stared at the ceiling. He felt ragged, but didn't think he'd be able to sleep. He'd been through far too much today for that kind of peace to find him – for any kind of peace to find him.

Forty-seven seconds later he was snoring quietly.

*

He awoke to the sound of a phone ringing. It was daylight outside, sunshine splashing in through the curtains. His eyes stung. He felt like he'd just closed them. His head felt like it was stuffed with broken glass and rusted screws – and now the phone was ringing. He cleared his throat and rubbed at his face and padded to the writing desk on the wall opposite and picked up the phone.

'Hello?'

'Checkout's in thirty.' He recognized the voice. It was the desk clerk he'd met last night.

'Oh. Okay. What time is it?'

'Half till ten.'

'Okay. Thank you.'

'Also,' the guy said – and Simon could tell from the tone that this was the real reason he'd called – 'and I know this ain't none of my business, but if you're wanted by the coppers, they found you.'

Suddenly there was no heartbeat in his chest, just silence and a sound like a desert wind. He swallowed. His heart started again.

'Excuse me?'

'Guy in a black Cadillac's been parked out front watching your car all morning. Looks like the fuzz to me.'

'Okay.'

He set the phone in its cradle.

He knew the man in the black Cadillac hadn't tailed him. He thought he knew that. He'd lost him last night before he was even half a mile from his house.

He pinched his eyes closed, and then opened them again.

The room didn't have its own shower – a hundred and forty bucks and no fucking shower – just a toilet and a sink. He needed to head back to Pasadena and get cleaned up and change clothes. He hoped Samantha was out. He didn't want to have to deal with her right now. He needed time to figure out what was happening. He also hoped the cops weren't staking the place out. Stabbing a guy in the arm wasn't murder. Nor was breaking into a business. Hopefully the cops had more important things to deal with. This wasn't a small town. Ten million people called Los Angeles County home. Out of that ten million people, thousands of them were surely capable of making much more trouble than he had created. Hopefully the cops were busy with them. Still – if it looked sketchy he'd forget about the shower and the change of clothes, but he needed to check it out.

But what was he going to do about the black Cadillac?

The guy wasn't a cop. The only reason for a cop to be following him before last night – before he'd stabbed Dr Zurasky and broken into his office – would be because the police knew he'd killed Jeremy Shackleford, and if the police had known that, they wouldn't have been following him. They would have been arresting him. Which meant the guy was working with – who? Not Zurasky. Zurasky wanted him in police custody, so if the guy was working for him, and he knew where Simon was, the police would be close behind. And since they weren't – well, who then?

Fuck it. For now he wasn't going to worry about it. After a few hours' sleep, it was less intimidating than last night. He'd let the son of a bitch follow him and see what happened.

As he drove he thought about seeing the dead walk. That didn't fit in with the Zurasky hypothesis. Unless somebody had drugged him and he'd hallucinated Müller and the dog. He'd seen them earlier and they'd stuck in his head because of their violent deaths and later he'd hallucinated them. Samantha had handed him pills she claimed were Tylenol. Perhaps they'd been something else altogether. He couldn't remember now if she gave him the pills before or after he'd seen the dead walking. Or maybe someone had replaced the blood thinners he had to take daily with something else – but then he last took those two nights ago. And if someone had replaced his blood thinners with some other drug, they'd done it before he had stepped into the role of Jeremy, and they'd known about his heart murmur, his caged-ball heart valve, the fact that he had to take pills daily, and that the best way to drug him was to slip those drugs into his bottle of blood thinners. But then whoever was orchestrating this had already demonstrated a thorough knowledge of both him and Shackleford, and the ability to get things done.

He simply couldn't wrap his brain around all this, he couldn't connect the dots. Maybe if he drank less. He'd had whiskey and wine and vodka throughout the day yesterday.

But this was making him feel panicky and lost and the booze calmed him. He hated this. He didn't know what to do at any moment, didn't know where to turn. He just had to take it one step at a time and hope he could untangle things – unfortunately they seemed to be more tangled than ever.

He parked two blocks from the house and walked the rest of the way. If cops were there, they might be looking for his car. The Cadillac pulled to the curb several car lengths behind him. The man behind the wheel did not step out into the sun. He just sat. Good.

Simon shivered as he walked through the sunshine of early fall.

After he turned the corner onto his street he paused. He looked down the length of the quiet suburban neighborhood and saw just that – a quiet suburban neighborhood. There was nothing out of the ordinary going on. Houses sat, lawns were green, and a gentle breeze ruffled eucalyptus leaves. That was all.

Samantha's car was not in the driveway. Maybe she was out at the police station filing yet another missing person report – or being questioned about where he might be as a result of last night's activities. Whatever she was doing she wasn't doing it here, and that suited Simon just fine.

As he keyed open the front door, someone behind him spoke.

'I really need that hammer, Jeremy.'

Simon jumped and turned around. The fat guy whose hammer Jeremy had – apparently – borrowed was jogging in place and looking at him.

'Now's a bad time.'

'I'm building a bookcase and I really need that hammer. That was my plan for the weekend.'

'What's today?'

'Tuesday.'

'Then it's not the weekend.'

Simon pulled open the front door and went inside without another word. He slammed the deadbolt home behind him.

The living room was cool and quiet. He had a strong urge to stretch out on the couch. He was still incredibly tired. He'd managed almost six hours of sleep, but that didn't seem to be enough. It took everything he had not to do it. Instead he walked down the hallway, through the master bedroom, and into the bathroom. He peeled away the layers of bloody sweat-stinking clothes and let them fall to the tiled floor, then stepped naked into the shower and turned on the water. It felt good to wash away the filth. The gauze covering his right hand got soaked, and he ended up pulling it away and dropping it to the shower floor. His wounds were no longer bleeding, anyway.

After drying off he walked to the bedroom and put on a gray suit. He put on a green tie, and the overcoat, and, still feeling cold, he wrapped a scarf around his neck.

Once dressed he walked to the living room. Since he was here he figured he might as well feed Francine. But she was gone.

After a moment's thought Simon decided he knew exactly where she was – and he wanted to go there anyway. There was a trunk he wanted to pry open.

The Volvo was gone. Maybe the police had taken it. Maybe they had gotten a warrant and taken it and were now searching it. Maybe they'd already searched it and had found Jeremy Shackleford's body in the trunk – his bones, anyway.

He shook his head at that thought. He didn't think that was it.

If the police had the car, and if Zurasky or someone working for him had planted Shackleford's body in its trunk, he wouldn't still be standing here. There'd be a dozen cops on him by now. Instead there were none. Someone else had the car.

Who?

He closed his eyes and rubbed at his forehead just above his left eyebrow. It throbbed with pain. He exhaled.

After a moment he opened his eyes again, decided he couldn't worry about that right now, and turned toward the back alley. He had locked the door last night when he left – creature of habit that he was – and had to break in.

He jumped up, grabbing for the ladder, but missed. He looked around for something to stand on. A broken cinder block leaned against the wall ten feet away. That might give him just enough added height. He grabbed it and set it beneath the ladder, stood atop it, and jumped again.

This time he managed to wrap a fist around the rusted fire-escape ladder and pull it down. Rust flakes fell around and on him. The third rung from the bottom fell right off the rusted ladder and onto the ground. He brushed himself down and then climbed the ladder, glad he'd only lived on the second floor.

He pushed the dead ficus on his fire escape aside with a dull-polished, scuff-toed shoe and climbed in through the bathroom window, trying to be as quiet as possible in case someone was here. How strange – having to break into his own apartment, having to worry about someone else lurking here.

His stomach felt tight. His head throbbed.

The apartment was hollow, a husk, a cocoon from which the moth had emerged. You could hear the dull hum of silence like tinnitus in your ear. Simon walked through this, feeling a slight droop as the floorboards gave beneath his weight.

As soon as he walked into the living room he saw it. The Mason jar sat atop the coffee table, Francine swimming inside.

He walked to the coffee table and picked up the jar. When he did he noticed something else: the picture of Shackleford and Samantha he had stolen was missing.

He strapped Francine into the passenger's seat and started the car. The black Cadillac was nowhere to be seen – when he'd walked back to the Saab in Pasadena, it had been gone. It bothered him that the guy had found him at that rat-hole motel in Hollywood. He knew he hadn't been followed there. He thought he knew he hadn't been followed there. But just lately he didn't know he knew anything.

No – two plus two still equaled four, and four plus four still equaled eight, and eight plus eight sixteen.

Some things could be depended upon.

Simon put the car into gear.

He would drop Francine off at the house in Pasadena and then figure out what his next move would be. Right now he didn't know what direction to turn in, what lead to follow. What he saw before him was a tangle, and no visible end piece with which to work.

He was on Virgil, heading toward Silver Lake Boulevard,

when the black Cadillac swept out of a side street and started tailing him again.

That's when he became certain his car had a transponder attached to it someplace. It should have been obvious to him this morning. It would have been if he were capable of thinking clearly. He needed to be able to think clearly. He needed to stop letting his emotions overwhelm him – the fear and the paranoia and the confusion. He needed to look at these events like a math problem. Instead he was letting each moment overwhelm him and acting on instinct and instinct wasn't—

He needed to lose the guy in the Cadillac and then pull into a parking lot or something and find the transponder on his car. The guy was tracking him for someone. He wasn't going to make a move; he would just continue to follow. And since Simon didn't know why, he didn't want it done. It didn't matter so much this morning – he'd just been going to take a shower, and the guy knew where Shackleford's house was already – but it would matter once he dropped off Francine and got to work on figuring this out. He didn't want anybody following him then.

Instead of continuing on toward home – toward Pasadena – he swung right onto Beverly Boulevard, made another right onto Rampart, and tried to lose the guy by turning randomly on a series of side streets just north of MacArthur Park. Unfortunately the guy didn't seem to care that Simon knew he was being followed – he tailed close –

and with traffic Simon found it impossible to get enough distance between him and the Cadillac to lose it.

Fine, then, if this guy wanted him so badly, Simon would make himself available. He was tired of being followed.

He led the Cadillac into a blind alley off Figueroa and slammed down on the brakes, screeching to a stop. Then he swung the driver's side door open and stepped outside.

'What do you want with me?' he said as he walked toward the Cadillac. 'What is it? I'm here. I'm right here. What the fuck do you want!?'

The jockey in the driver's seat looked left and then right, seemingly in a panic. It was hard to be sure, his eyes were impossible to see through the black lenses of his sunglasses, but his movements made it look to Simon like he was in a panic, squirming in his seat.

And then the guy put the Cadillac into reverse and screeched backwards down the alleyway. His left front fender banged against a brick wall and he lost a side-view mirror, and then he screeched into the street. A car horn blared. Brakes squealed. Metal crunched and the Cadillac spun in a half circle.

The car that hit it was a yellow Gremlin, and after a moment a heavy-set Hispanic woman stepped from it and started storming toward the jockey saying, 'You stupid motherfucker. What the fuck do you think you're fucking doing!? I'm gonna call my husband, he's gonna kick your fucking—'

The jockey put the Cadillac into gear and it roared away.

'Where the fuck do you think you're—'

She threw her cell phone at the car and it bounced off the back window and then shattered against the asphalt.

'Fuck!' she said.

It was tucked under the right-front wheel well, a simple black box with a red light on one end. It blinked steadily. Simon threw it to the ground and then stepped into the car. He started the engine and was backing out of the alley when he realized that Francine was missing. The seatbelt was still snapped into place but there was no Mason jar there under the strap.

He stepped out of the car, looked around, and saw no one. The alleyway was empty.

The jar was sitting on the coffee table when he walked back into the apartment on Wilshire.

Instead of driving back to the house to drop off Francine he drove directly to the Pasadena College of the Arts. He had wasted enough of his day chasing Francine around and he wanted to get Kate Wilhelm's address so he could pay her a visit. She knew something and he wanted to get it out of her. She knew something about his past and how it was connected with Jeremy Shackleford – something he couldn't remember. And he was becoming more and more certain that everything revolved around that something. He couldn't see it but he knew it was there the same way scientists knew of a planet they couldn't see: by its gravitational effect on everything around it that they *could* see. Everything seemed to revolve around this invisible part of his past. His past and Jeremy Shackleford's.

He walked through the parking lot, carrying Francine, and thinking about that. Something had happened last May and he couldn't remember it. Kate knew what it was, and who he was. She had called him Simon and she knew he couldn't remember last May. That had to be where he was connected with Shackleford, the point at which their paths had first crossed. Samantha had said that Jeremy'd had an accident last year. She didn't say it had been in May but Simon now knew it had been. It had to have been.

He was digging through desk drawers, pulling out stacks of papers and flipping through them, looking for Kate's information, when Howard Ullman knocked on the office door and then pushed his way in without waiting for a response.

'I thought I heard you in here.'

'Hi.'

'Samantha's been in a panic. She called four times to

see if you'd come in to work. The cops have had her at the station all morning, asking her questions she doesn't know the answers to. You missed your algebra class. What the hell is going on?'

'I'm in the middle of something. Can this wait?'

'You're in the middle of something?'

'Yes.'

'A nervous breakdown perhaps?'

'I can't explain it.'

'Does it involve Kate Wilhelm?'

Simon looked up and really examined Ullman's face for the first time since he'd walked in. He was unshaven. His lips were chapped and there was a bloody scab on the bottom one where he had scraped away at the dead skin with his teeth. His eyes were marijuana-reddened but sharp with intelligence and perception and Simon didn't like the shine they had at all.

'Why – ' he licked his lips – 'what makes you think that?'

'I can't think of what else it might be.'

'But what would it have to do with Kate Wilhelm?'

Ullman was quiet for a minute. He ran his tongue over his teeth, sucked at something stuck behind his eyetooth, swallowed.

'You've not been yourself,' he said finally. 'You need to get help. I don't think you can save your job at this point. Carol has it in for you – and at this point I'm way past defending your behavior. But you might – just maybe – be able to save your marriage. Samantha loves you. She's put up with more than any woman in her right mind would. You're lucky for that. But I don't think she's gonna put up with much more, Jeremy. In fact, I won't let her. If you fuck up again, I'll have to rip out your heart.'

'What?'

'I don't want Samantha to have to watch you fall apart.'

Ullman left without answering any of his questions.

He continued digging through paperwork for another twenty minutes but mostly what he found were absences. He didn't have a Wilhelm in any of his classes, for instance. No Kate or Kathryn or Kathy or Katrina – no Wilhelm at all. But while he looked for Kate's information, he also hoped to find something else that might be useful. He knew more now than when he'd first searched the office, so maybe now something that meant nothing then would be of significance. He found no reference to himself. He found no reference to Zurasky. He found one reference to Kate – if it was the same Kate, and he thought it was – the beginning of a letter addressed to her that had been crumpled and shoved into a desk drawer unfinished.

Kate: I know this is difficult for you. It's not easy for me either. That said, you simply cannot continue down this path. You're angry, I hurt you, but that

was never my intention. I always told you there was
no future in this. I tried in every way I knew how
to make sure you knew this would never be love.

If you continue down this path, you're going
to end up hurting yourself as much as you hurt me –
perhaps more. I know you said you never wanted to
see me again, but I'd like to talk to you in person.
Maybe we can

That was the whole thing. It was written on a sheet of yellow paper in blue ink. There was a coffee stain on the bottom right-hand side, and the word

FUCK

was scrawled in big letters across the two paragraphs.

He folded it up and slipped it into a pocket. Then he grabbed Francine from the top of the desk and headed toward his car in the parking lot.

As he reached the Saab and unlocked the car door he realized his hands were empty. He was almost certain he'd grabbed Francine from the desk before walking out of the office – almost. He could close his eyes and remember the way he'd reached across the desk, the way his hip had bumped a stack of papers and knocked it down, the way the papers spread across the floor like a fanned deck of cards, the feel of the cool glass against his fingertips hard and smooth – and yet his hands were empty.

The jar wasn't in the office.

He knew he was wasting time, but he couldn't stop himself.

He parked the car on the south side of Wilshire, in front of the Korean barbecue joint, and jogged across the street toward the Filboyd Apartments, dodging a smattering of cars as he went.

The man in the Cadillac, the jockey, was parked on the north side of the street, in front of his building, watching him through the black lenses of his sunglasses. Had he known Simon was going to come back here or had it been a lucky guess? Had he taken the jar knowing that Simon would—

Maybe he was being followed by more than one person. He couldn't see the jockey's eyes. He was pretending to examine the backs of his fingers, nibbling at bloody hangnails there, but Simon knew the man was really watching him.

He pushed his way through the front doors before he remembered he had no key to get in, pushed his way back out, and walked around the corner of the building toward the fire escape in back. As he walked up the sidewalk toward the alleyway he saw Helmut Müller. The man was walking toward him, looking down at his feet, making small steps and watching the sidewalk like if he didn't stay focused he'd forget what he was doing. Maybe he would. Death was a pretty good excuse for a bad memory. When he heard Simon's footsteps he looked up at him.

'Well, take him,' Müller said, then looked past Simon's shoulder and nodded.

Simon looked behind him, saw nothing. Then he walked past Müller without a word and into the alley.

The Mason jar was resting on the coffee table and Francine was swimming inside it. He picked it up and started back to the bathroom. The man in the Cadillac was out on Wilshire right now, probably putting another transponder under one of his wheel wells. He'd had enough of that son of a bitch.

He walked into the bathroom and crawled back out through the open window. With Francine tucked into his armpit, snuggled under his right arm like an infant, he made his way precariously down the ladder. Once at the bottom he looked around the alley for a weapon. The cinder block was too large and awkward. Nothing else seemed remotely intimidating. He was about to give up when, turning in a circle to see what the alley contained, his foot kicked something metal. A rusty rung knocked from the fire escape lay on the ground amongst a thatch of weeds growing up through a crack in the asphalt. He vaguely remembered it falling there. He picked it up and felt it for weight.

Nodding to himself – it was good and heavy, and rust had decayed one end to a sharp point – he walked out of the alley.

He walked all the way around the block so that he could come up behind the Cadillac and the jockey would remain unaware of his presence unless he happened to glance in his rear-view mirror. But he would be looking for Simon to come out the front of the building or around the corner, so Simon remained hopeful. About a half block behind the car was the bench that sat in front of Captain Bligh's. Simon set Francine down beneath it, pushing the jar against the wall so no one would kick it over.

'Wait here.'

Then he continued toward the black Cadillac and the man inside. The metal gripped in his fist felt grimy and was turning his palm a reddish orange. His hands were moist with sweat. His mouth was dry. He walked carefully and smoothly forward. The sounds of the cars and trucks driving by on Wilshire faded away. The world seemed very clear and clean and crisp, like it did after rain. He walked out into the street, continuing onward. He raised the pipe in his right hand up over his shoulder.

As he walked past the left rear fender the jockey glanced him in his side-view mirror, slammed a hand down on the door lock, and tried to roll up the window. But he was too late. Simon reached through and grabbed him by the collar of his thin black sport coat and fought him bodily through the window. Once more of him was outside the car than inside, Simon let him go, and gravity threw him to the street.

A car in the right lane had to swerve to miss him, and its driver laid on the horn.

The man scrambled out of the street, crawling backwards in a crabwalk toward the curb, between the front of his Cadillac and the bumper-sticker-covered red Toyota parked in front of it.

Simon walked toward him with the rusty pipe in his hand, heart pounding in his chest.

'Wait,' the jockey said. 'You don't wanna do that. You do *not* wanna do that. Just wait. Wait wait – wait.'

'Who are you and why are you following me?'

'I don't – I don't know what you're talking about. I—'

Simon swung the pipe down and slammed it against the jockey's left knee.

He let out a scream.

'Why are you following me?'

'I don't—' turned into another scream as Simon hit him again.

'Who are you?'

'I—'

'Take off your glasses.'

'What?'

'Take them off. I wanna see your eyes.'

'I don't know—'

Simon smashed the pipe against the jockey's neck. It left an orange rust stain on his flesh. He screamed in pain, grabbing at the point of contact with pale fingers. There was dirt under his fingernails and they were surrounded by the pink gashes of torn-away hangnails.

'I'm not gonna let you lie to me. Let me see your eyes. I want to know you're telling me the truth.'

'I can't take them off.'

Simon raised the pipe again.

The guy held up his hands. The palms were dirty and small pebbles were embedded in the meat of them from his crawl away from Simon.

'Okay. Okay, okay – okay.'

Simon waited.

The jockey let out a sigh. He rubbed at his neck. It was welting and turning red beneath the rusted orange. He swallowed. His throat made a dry clicking sound when he did.

Simon noticed for the first time that they weren't standard sunglasses he was wearing. They were flying goggles, a leather strap wrapping them around the jockey's head.

'Take them off.'

'I am.'

'I won't say it again.'

'I'm taking them off.'

Finally he reached to the glasses with both hands and pulled the lenses up onto his forehead.

His eyes became slits as he squinted in the sunlight. A gasp escaped his mouth. Pink tears – part blood and part water – streamed down his cheeks. His eyes were nothing but tiny black pupils floating in a sea of white, like a single dot on an otherwise blank page. With no color in their centers the whites of the eyes seem unbelievably white, like snow-covered mountainsides through which no black rocks or treetops were jutting.

Suddenly Simon remembered what Chris had told him about UFOs and the travelers who came here within them. They got crazy eyes. He hadn't gotten to say what their eyes looked like before Robert cut him off but—

It couldn't be true – could it? It had to be bullshit. And yet—

At this point he was ready to believe anything.

'Are you – are you one of them?'

'What? One of who?'

'Where do you come from?'

'Where do I – Culver City. Well, just east of Culver City. Near Washington and La Brea.'

'No – where are you from originally?'

'I don't—'

'Stop stalling!'

'Ohio. All right? I don't know what you want from me.'

'You were born in Ohio?'

'Yeah.'

'What city?'

'Westerville.'

'Westerville a big town?'

'No.'

'What's the population?'

'I – uh – it was about thirty thousand when I left.'

'When was that?'

'Ninety-seven.'

'Nineteen ninety-seven?'

'No, eighteen ninety-seven.'

Simon raised the pipe in his hand.

'Yes! Yes – nineteen ninety-seven.'

'You're not one of them?'

'I don't know what you're talk—'

'Fine. Why are you following me?'

'I'm a private investigator.'

'What's wrong with your eyes?'

'Lack of pigment. I was born that way.'

'Your hair's black.'

'Localized to the eyes.'

'What's that called?'

'What's what called?'

'When you have albino eyes.'

'I don't know.' He wiped at the bloody pink water running down his face. 'It's a long name. I can never remember.'

'And you're not one of them?'

'I don't know what that means.'

'Who hired you?'

'Can I put the glasses—'

'No. Who hired you?'

'I can't tell you that. Client privilege. It wouldn't be right.'

'Who fucking hired you?'

'Listen—'

Simon slammed the pipe down onto the man's shoulder and it let out a sick ring so low in tone it was barely a ring at all. The man let out a yelp and rubbed at the orange stain on his black coat.

'I already gave you three chances. I'm gonna give you one more. That's more than you'd get in baseball.'

'Your wife.'

Simon nodded. He wasn't surprised. He didn't think anything the man said would surprise him. If the guy had admitted to being one of them, Simon thought he would have believed that – believed it and gone on from there.

'Why did she hire you?'

'I don't know.'

'Don't lie to me.'

'I'm not. She didn't say. She just said she wanted me to follow you, keep track of where you were going, tell her what I saw. I assumed she suspected another woman, but she didn't say so, so I don't know.'

'You're fired.'

Simon tossed the rusty pipe away.

'Is there a transponder on my car?'

The jockey hesitated.

'Where is it?'

'Right front wheel well.'

'You put it in the same place twice?'

The guy shrugged.

'I figured you'd look everywhere but the same spot.'

'Keep whatever retainer my wife gave you, but don't let me see you again.'

'Okay.'

The man pulled the goggles back down over his eyes.

When Simon went back to get Francine she was gone.

He was halfway down the rusted fire-escape ladder when he realized his arm was empty.

He stopped, holding onto a rung, and considered climbing back up to get her, but he knew what would happen – the same thing that'd been happening all day.

It was a distraction. He had to let her go. Chasing after his goddamn goldfish was not getting him any closer to finding out what was happening. Besides, he was no longer certain she was real.

'Sorry, Francine.'

He continued down the fire escape.

*

He yanked the wheel to the right and the Saab rolled up the curb and onto a strip of lawn growing between the curb and the sidewalk before screeching to a stop, grass tearing beneath a tire, revealing moist black soil and the insects and worms that lived within. He pushed open the driver's side door and stepped out into the day. He felt tense. Samantha had hired a private detective to follow him. She had given him pills and – if he was remembering correctly – he had hallucinated shortly thereafter. Or had he hallucinated before? He couldn't remember now. He had certainly been hallucinating since. Helmut Müller was dead. That stray dog was dead. The thing with the goldfish was just weird.

He pushed his way through the front door.

'Samantha?'

Silence.

'Samantha?'

Faint, from the bathroom: 'Jeremy?'

'Yeah.'

'Hold on.'

The sound of the toilet flushing, water running, the door opening.

Samantha emerged from the hallway with damp hands. She wiped them back then front on her shirt.

'Where have you been? The police came by looking for you. Did you *stab* Dr Zurasky?'

'What are you doing to me?'

'What?'

'You had someone following me.'

'Calm down.'

'You had someone *following* me.'

'Jeremy, I – I didn't.'

'I'm not asking. I'm telling you I know you did.'

'But – listen.'

'Okay.' He crossed his arms. 'I'm listening.'

'Okay.'

She opened her mouth but nothing came out. She looked jumpy and alarmed. Her eyes searched his face, he knew not what for. She licked her lips nervously, swallowed.

'I—'

'Yes?'

'I – I did it for your own good, Jeremy. I didn't want you to disappear again.'

'My own good?'

'Fine. If that's not acceptable, how about *my* own good – my sanity? I did it so I would know where you were, so I would know you were safe, so I would know—'

'What is it to you where I am?'

'I'm your wife.'

'Are you?'

Simon took a step forward; Samantha took a step back.

'What are you doing?'

'That's my question for you. What are you doing? Have you been drugging me?'

'What?'

'Have you?'

'No. Of course I—'

'Not that you would admit it even if you were.'

He took another step forward, she took another step back.

'Don't do this, Jeremy. You're scaring me.'

'Then tell me what's happening to me.'

'I don't know,' Samantha said. 'If I did, don't you think I'd stop it?'

Simon tongued the inside of his cheek and simply looked at her.

Finally he said, 'How would I know what you'd do? I don't even know you.'

'What do you mean?'

He turned back toward the door.

That's when he saw it.

There was a framed photograph sitting on an end table. Simon recognized it. It was the photograph he'd stolen from the house on that day he'd first sneaked in. It felt like that had happened years ago rather than just over two weeks ago. There were Samantha and Jeremy standing side by side. Samantha's arm was through Jeremy's. Jeremy was wearing a suit Simon had worn himself. And he recognized the background – he knew where the picture'd been taken. Two weeks ago he hadn't, but he did now.

He picked it up and looked at it for a long moment.

'Where – where did this come from?'

Samantha was holding herself and looking at him with sadness.

'That woman Marlene Biskind brought it by about twenty minutes ago. It was one of the pictures she took at my show last night and she thought I might want to have it.'

Simon looked from her to the picture in his hand. He could feel it shaking.

'This is,' he licked his lips, 'this is a picture of me?'

'Who else would it be a picture of?'

He pulled the Saab's driver's side door open.

'I really need that hammer, Jeremy.'

Simon spun around.

He wasn't jogging now. He was wearing slacks and a tucked-in T-shirt.

Simon pulled out his – Jeremy's – wallet and looked inside. He grabbed a hundred-dollar bill and thrust it forward.

'Here. Just buy a hammer.'

'I don't want to buy a hammer. I loaned you a hammer and I want it back.'

'It's a hundred dollars.'

'I just want my hammer.'

'Fine. I'll get your fucking hammer.'

He slammed the car door shut and stormed toward the house, flung the door open, and started digging around, looking for a hammer in various drawers. He didn't find one, but he found a Stanley screwdriver, thought he could use it to switch his license plates, keep the cops off him for a while longer, and stuffed it into his overcoat pocket. Then he continued searching.

'What are you doing?'

'Looking for a hammer.'

Samantha disappeared and a moment later emerged from the garage with one.

'This hammer?'

He took it from her without a word and walked back outside, holding it up.

'Is this the hammer you want?' He felt suddenly furious. Rage flushed his cheeks. His chest felt tight. His brain was boiling with anger and thoughtless. 'Is this the fucking hammer you want?'

'What other hammer would I—'

Simon swung it down against the side of the son of a bitch's head.

'There's your fucking hammer.'

The guy collapsed to the ground screaming and holding his face. Simon let go of the hammer and it dropped to the driveway and then bounced onto the lawn. After a moment blood began to pour from between the man's fingers and into the grass. The guy flailed about on his side, staining his jeans and his T-shirt with grass. Neighbors walked from their front doors, asking if everything was okay, wondering if—

Simon got into his car, mumbling under his breath. He was tired of everyone coming at him. He was tired of feeling frantic and lost and not knowing what direction to turn. And everyone coming at him. Samantha. That private detective. Zurasky. And that son of a bitch and his fucking hammer. Goddamn them all.

He drove the car off the curb, and screeched away from there.

He drove around the Fillmore train station parking lot till he found a spot, parked his car, and got out. He dug the screwdriver from his overcoat's inside pocket and walked to the Ford Explorer beside which he'd just parked. Glancing left and then right, he sat on his haunches and began unscrewing the plates.

He drove along Hollywood Boulevard, past Grauman's Chinese Theater and the Ripley's museum. There was a crowd in front of the theater.

A cop car drove by going in the opposite direction. Simon's chest tightened but the cop didn't even glance at him.

It felt strange. How could he feel so guilty – how could he be so guilty: of killing a man and trying to dispose of the body, of breaking and entering, of two assaults – and not draw the attention of every officer of the law within a hundred miles? Especially when everything was falling apart. It seemed the natural progression, the next step, and yet—

He stuck a cigarette between his dry lips as he drove and reached for his Zippo. It was gone. He had lost it. He thumbed in the car's built-in lighter and after a few moments it popped back out. He lighted his cigarette and inhaled deeply. The smoke made his lungs feel like over-filled balloons, taut and ready to pop.

He exhaled.

As he drove he tried to wrap his mind around the events of the last couple weeks. He tried to put the clues in some kind of working order. He tried to untangle the ugly, messy knot of events. He couldn't do it. But as he neared the motel – beige stucco with gray patches of concrete where the exterior had recently been repaired after, from the look of the damage, a car had been driven into the manager's office – something clicked. And while it didn't make sense of everything, it gave him something to work with.

Walk the mile. Well, take him.

Yeah, he had something to work with.

He hoped he did.

'You're back,' the guy behind the counter said, then he grabbed a hair from his nostril, plucked it, examined it, and threw it to the floor.

'I am. But I'd like it if you could forget you ever saw me.'

'Not a problem. You gotta be forgetful around here.'

Simon nodded.

'You ditch the fuzz?'

'Wasn't the police. Private investigator.'

'Marital trouble?'

'What do you know about it?'

'Nothing, man. Just conversatin'.'

'Anyways, you got a pen or a marker or something I could write with?'

The guy dug a black marker from a coffee mug and set it on the counter.

'How long you staying for this time? I can give you a discount if it's three days or more.'

'I don't know how long. We'll take it day by day.'

'Suit yourself.'

Simon paid and the guy gave him his key. It was for the same room he'd had last night. One thirteen: bad luck plus one. He was at the manager's door – looking out into the parking lot – when he stopped and turned around.

'If anybody asks, who stayed in my room?'

'Blond fellow with a harelip. Had a birthmark on his neck shaped like Texas.'

'Unfortunate fellow.'

'Most folks are who end up here – their days of shitting in tall cotton far behind 'em. If they ever had any of those days to begin with.' He looked sad and contemplative.

Simon nodded and held up the marker. 'I'll bring this back when I'm done.'

When he couldn't find paper he wrote both phrases on the wall.

> Walk the mile
> Well, take him

One a, two e's, one h, one i, one k, two l's, one m, one t, one w – same letters for both of them. They were anagrams – just as he'd thought. But what else? He stared at them for a long time, those phrases scrawled in his shaking hand on the lumpy motel-room wall, illuminated by pale yellow lamplight. When was the last time he'd eaten? His stomach felt empty and sour and was grumbling and boiling. Could stomachs consume themselves?

This wasn't the time to think about that. He could eat later.

Anagrams.

After a while he started writing, slowly at first, but gaining speed as he continued on, as he got the hang of it:

> We Hamlet ilk
> Lathe, we milk
> Elm wheal kit
> Whale elm kit

Whale me kilt
Ahem, wet kill
Make hell, wit
Make wet hill
Tweak him, Ell
Wake them ill
Weak, tell him
I, metal whelk
Hew metal ilk
Helm, wale kit
Hall wet, Mike
Hat well, Mike
Me talk while
Walk them, lie
The lime walk
Hawk, I tell me
Halt 'em, we ilk
He law me kilt
Hi, law elk, met
Mew, at he, kill
At hem we kill

He chewed on his bottom lip as he wrote, one ana-
gram after another, none of them making the least bit of
sense to him, though he paused after a couple, and stared,
trying to make them mean something. He couldn't do it,
though, and so he continued on – writing away.

Then he stopped again and sat on the bed.

He looked at his collection of nonsensical anagrams. He could think of another dozen, no problem – maw hike tell, aw theme kill, ha me well kit, math like Lew, and on and on – but saw no point in writing them down when they meant nothing to him.

He threw the marker against the wall, watched it fall to the floor, and fell back on the mattress. He stared at the ceiling. It was covered in spray-on texture – what he'd called popcorn ceiling as a kid – except in one section. That section looked like it had been recently repaired. Maybe there had been a roof leak and the rotten section had been cut out and replaced. Or maybe—

He sat up, got to his feet, picked up the marker, and wrote two words on the wall at the end of his list:

Kate Wilhelm

One a, two e's, one h, one i, one k, two l's, one m, one t, one w – Kate Wilhelm. He stared at the two words for a long time. It should have been obvious. If he'd been able to think clearly it would have been.

He thought of the letter Jeremy Shackleford had written to her.

What had she done? He had said she couldn't continue on this path. He had said she would end up hurting herself as much as she hurt him. How had she hurt him? What had she done?

'You thought I was too stupid to figure out it was you.' He licked his lips. 'You won't think I'm so stupid now.'

He sat at the writing desk in the corner of the room, picked up the telephone, and dialed 4–1–1.

'City and state, please.'

'Los Angeles, California.'

'How can I help you, sir?'

'The number for a Kate Wilhelm.'

'Wilhelm?'

'Wilhelm.' He spelled it for her.

'Okay, sir, there's twenty-three results for Wilhelm but no Kate.'

'Is there a K?'

'No, sir. It goes from John to Mack.'

Simon was silent.

'Sir?'

'Would it be possible to get them all?'

'All twenty-three, sir?'

'Yeah.'

A sigh.

'Do you have a pen and paper, sir?'

'I have a marker.'

'Okay, sir. This first one is Amanda.'

'Okay.'

He took down names and numbers, scribbling them upon the wood surface of the writing desk since he didn't have a piece of paper, the meat of his hand just below the pinky occasionally smearing a last name or the last four digits of a phone number as he dragged his hand over it. Eventually he had them all.

He hung up the phone. He turned around, looking over his shoulder at the digital clock on the night stand. The red numbers claimed it was

$$8:54$$

It was still early enough to call.

He turned back around and looked at the phone. He had a knot in his stomach. For some reason this filled him with dread, with a vague fear that had no direction to turn, that had no focus at all. He swallowed and looked at that first number.

He had to do it so he might as well just get on with it.

He picked up the phone and dialed.

'Hello?'

'Hi, is Kate there?'

'Kate?'

'Kate Wilhelm.'

'What number are you calling?'

He told her.

'Right number,' the woman on the other end of the line said, 'wrong person.'

'Okay. Sorry to bother you.'

'No bother.' Click.

Keeping the phone to his ear, he severed the line with his left hand, dropping his first two fingers on the button, then lifted his hand, listened to the dial tone, and dialed the next number. He got a similar response – on and on he got that response. Sorry, no, wrong number, nobody here by that name, who are you trying to call, I don't know anyone by that name, huh-uh, nope, bye.

That was how it went until he got to John Wilhelm.

'Yeah?'

'Hi. Is uh—'

'What?'

'Is Kate there?'

Silence.

'Hello?'

Finally: 'Is this some kind of joke?'

'No, sir.'

'Who is this?'

'Excuse me?'

'Who's calling?'

'Is – is Kate there?'

'I said, who's calling?'

'Simon.'

'When was the last time you saw Kate, Simon?'

'It's – it's been a while.'

More silence.

'Hello?'

'Kate's dead.'

'What?'

'Dead.'

'When?'

'Last April.'

'That's not – when?'

'Last April, I said.'

He didn't respond. Eventually the guy on the other end of the line grew impatient with the silence: 'Hello?'

'That's not possible.'

'I'm afraid it is. Goodbye.'

Then the sound of the line being severed. Simon sat with the phone pressed against his ear for some time. Eventually a recorded voice broke through the silence. 'If you would like to make a call, please hang up and—'

He set the phone in its cradle, looked down at his lap, thinking about what to do next, and then picked it up again and again dialed 4–1–1.

'City and state, please.'

'Los Angeles, California,' he said. 'I need the address for a John Wilhelm.'

'There's no John Wilhelm in Los Angeles, sir, but there's one in Burbank.'

'That's the one.'

In the dream he was driving a yellow Chevy Nova, and though he was not a particularly tall man – five foot nine – his knees were brushing against the steering wheel. The seat was adjusted for a shorter person. This was not his car.

He saw blood on his hands as they gripped the wheel, in the creases of his skin, under his thumbnails. He glanced to his right, but the passenger's seat was empty.

That didn't make sense; he knew Kate was in the car.

He turned his head to look in the back seat and saw—

Someone banging on the door awoke him. He didn't know where, when, or who he was. He looked around to reorient himself with his surroundings. He had fallen asleep in the chair at the writing desk. He'd decided to go pay John Wilhelm a visit, put his face into his hands and closed his eyes, just for a minute, just to think about how he'd handle the situation, and must have fallen asleep. His neck was killing him.

How long had he slept?

'Open up, motherfucker!'

The banging continued.

He rubbed at his eyes with his knuckles, looked out of the window. His eyes itched. It was night. The clock said it was nine forty-five. He wondered if an entire day had passed. He didn't think so. He thought it was still Tuesday. It *had* been Tuesday, right? He just couldn't think at—

'I'll kick this fucking door down!'

'Who is it?'

'Open the fucking door I know she's in there.' The words slurred together.

'There's no she in here at all.'

'Open the fucking door and prove it.'

Simon walked to the door and pulled it open as far as the chain would allow. He looked out and saw a praying-mantis-looking guy in a wife-beater and cargo shorts. He was bare-footed. The guy looked at him with confusion.

'Who the fuck are you?'

'The guy whose door you've been banging on.'

'What room—' He looked at the number on the door. 'Man, this is the wrong fucking room.' He said it in a tone that suggested Simon had made the mistake: he'd obviously put his room in the wrong spot. The guy walked away shaking his head.

Simon shut the door.

A moment later he heard banging on someone else's.

'Open up. I know she's in there!'

Simon was glad the guy'd woken him up. He had to pay someone a visit.

Steering with his knee as he drove, he stuck a cigarette between his lips and lighted it (this time with motel matches; he couldn't believe he'd lost his lighter on top of everything else). Then he pressed a button on the door and the window hummed and slid down a couple of inches. A breeze blew against his face. Traffic was light but the noise of humming tires was loud.

The lights of the city flickered to his left like grounded stars.

The house was small and dark – nearly all the lights inside turned off. Only one room's window glowed with a dim yellow light, like a jack-o'-lantern. The yard was flat and bare, no flowers or trees or shrubbery of any kind, just a lawn littered with crabgrass and dandelions. The stucco looked dull and unpainted. It was just concrete gray. A light blue Ford Pinto station wagon sat in the driveway, the back window shattered, replaced by a black trash bag which was held in place by now-peeling duct tape, crisped by the sun. The tags on the license plate were eight months past expiration.

He pulled to a stop at the curb and stepped out into the night. He dropped his cigarette into the gutter. The flame was snuffed out by a slow trickle of water coming from someone's sprinkling system several houses down. The sound of freeway traffic echoed through the cul-de-sac. A cool breeze tousled his hair. He swallowed.

Finally, after simply standing for several long moments, he walked across the lawn – feeling dead grass crunch beneath the soles of his feet despite the moisture of the soil in which it was rooted – and when he reached the front door he knocked.

There was silence from within – and then the sound of

footsteps nearing the door, the rattle of the doorknob being turned, the pained moan of sore hinges.

And then a man in his forties was looking at Simon. He was barrel-chested and bare-chested, wearing only a pair of canvas shorts. His torso was covered in a thick layer of hair in which crumbs of food were nestled. His hair was brown except at the temples, which were gray, and his beard – which was long and tangled – matched his temples. The crow's feet at the corners of his eyes cut deep lines into his flesh. He was holding a can of Budweiser. His eyes were dull as he opened the door but when he finally got around to looking at Simon they went sharp and bright and angry.

'What the fuck are you doing here?'

'I'm – what?'

'Why are you here?'

'I'm—' Simon swallowed. 'I'm here to see Kate. Is she here?'

'What?'

'I'm here to—'

'*You* called me earlier tonight.'

'What? No.'

Simon didn't know why he lied. It was simply his first instinct. When someone asks you if you did something and he's got an accusatory tone in his voice you say no.

'I recognize your voice. I thought it sounded familiar.'

'You're right. I'm sorry. I called. I just want to see Kate. I don't know what she told you, but I really—'

'What she told me? Are you out of your mind? Kate is dead.'

'That's what you said on the phone, but I—'

'But nothing. What did you come here for?'

The man – John – now had moisture in his eyes, and they were going red. He blinked several times quickly and looked away at something in the corner.

'She can't have died last April. I saw her yesterday.'

'Just get out of here.'

'Maybe I can come in and look aro—'

'No. I told you at the inquest I never wanted to see your fucking face again and I meant it. In fact, if I recall, I told you I'd kill you if I ever saw you again, and you're really tempting me. Get off my lawn. Get out of here. Never come back.'

'But she can't be—'

'She *is*!' John yelled. 'And you fucking know it. I don't know what the fuck is wrong with you and I don't care. Now *leave*!'

As he said the last word he pulled back and threw his can of Budweiser. It was almost full and when it slammed against Simon's chest from only three or four feet away it knocked the wind out of him. He stumbled backwards and then fell on his ass on the lawn.

The can dropped to the front porch and vomited foaming liquid from its metal mouth while rolling along the gentle grade toward the grass.

*

An image like a shard of glass cut through his mind: a yellow Chevy Nova smashing through a guardrail. There were trees thirty or forty feet below, growing on the edge of a cliff, and in a moment, once gravity kicked in, the car would be dropped into them.

As the Nova flew through the air its front end tilted downward, the headlights splashing across the tops of trees, and from where he sat in the passenger's seat, Simon could see a flock of birds take flight from one of them, frightened by the sound of the car's engine.

He glanced to his left, to the driver's seat, and—

'Was it a car accident?'

Simon looked up from the lawn toward John Wilhelm. The man looked back at him momentarily and then without a word slammed the door shut. That was followed by the sound of a lock clicking into place. Apparently he wasn't going to answer that question.

Simon got to his feet and dusted himself off. His ass was wet from the grass, his chest wet with beer.

He walked to the car and got inside.

When he got back to his room he found the thermostat and turned on the heater – a small, rusty radiator that looked like an accordion. The night air had chilled him to the bone – that and the moisture from the grass, and the beer which poured down the front of his shirt – despite the overcoat and scarf he had on. With the heater on, he sat at the wood chair in front of the writing desk and picked up the telephone. He dialed 4–1–1.

'City and state, please.'

'Glendale, California.'

'How can I help you?'

'Christopher Watkins.'

'One minute, sir.'

'Okay.'

There was the sound of fingers tapping away at a keyboard.

'I have it, sir. Would you like me to connect you?'

'Yes, please.'

Silence as if the line had been severed, then a dial tone, and then the phone began ringing. It rang four and a half times.

'Hello?'

The voice sounded groggy, full of phlegm.

'Did I wake you?'

'Simon?'

'Yeah.'

'Hey, man, what's going on? It's like eleven-thirty.'

'Sorry.'

'It's all right. What's up?'

'I need to ask you something.'

'Ask away.'

'When you watched the special about UFOs – what did

it say about the eyes?' Simon knew he was grasping at straws, but ever since he left Burbank that private detective had been on his mind and he couldn't figure out why, but something in the back of his mind had put him and Kate together in some way.

'What are you talking about?'

'The UFO special you mentioned. On TV.'

'Oh, that's on tomorrow night.'

'What are you talking about? We talked about it at lunch over two weeks ago.'

'Nope.'

'Is it a repeat?'

'No, man, they been pushing this thing like it's cocaine. It's brand new.'

'That doesn't – okay. I gotta go.'

He put the phone into its cradle.

'Bye,' he said to the empty room.

He walked to a liquor store on the corner and bought a bottle of whiskey. He drank it and watched TV till very late. He wondered if when this was over he might be able to get his old job back. He'd not called Mr Thames again after that first time. He was certain he'd been fired. But maybe he could get his old job back. He'd been a very good employee right up until—

He walked to the phone and dialed the office number and the extension and got the answering service. He rambled into the phone for a while and then hung up. He walked to the bed and lay down and by the time he was asleep he didn't even remember he had done it.

He woke up with two things – a hangover, and the knowledge of where the private detective and Kate fit together. The guy'd been tailing him on Monday night when he met up with the woman impersonating Kate Wilhelm. If she really was dead. Maybe it had been her. Maybe Mr Wilhelm had been lying. He didn't seem to be, but—

He'd remember it. The detective. And if it was someone impersonating Kate, maybe he knew something about her real identity.

He grabbed his keys and headed out.

He unlocked the front door and stepped quietly into the foyer. He hadn't seen any cop cars, unmarked cars, or anything that seemed suspiciously out of place, but even so, he wouldn't have been surprised to find cops waiting for him. They weren't. It was almost disappointing.

Samantha's car was in the driveway, but the living room was quiet and empty.

Her purse was sitting on the couch.

He walked to it and started digging through it, looking for that private detective's business card.

'Jeremy?'

He looked up. Samantha was standing in the entrance to the hallway in a pink silk nightgown, arms wrapped around her body. Her hair was a tangle and her make-up was smeared – she must have gone to bed without washing her face – but she still looked beautiful.

'Where is it?'

'What are you doing?'

'His business card. Where is it?'

'What are you talking about?'

'The private detective you hired to follow me. I need to talk to him.'

'Why?'

He threw the purse to the ground.

'Just tell me where he is!'

The detective's name was Adam Posniak and he had an office in a street-front strip of beige stucco on Washington Boulevard just east of La Brea. Simon pulled the Saab into the gray asphalt parking lot, found a spot, and slipped the car into it.

He recognized the car to his left. It was a black Cadillac, dented up from a recent accident.

The private detective's office was between a barbecue place and a manicure–pedicure place. There was no sign on the tattered green awning above it. The door said only

SUITE 12D

no name, and the glass was soaped so you couldn't see inside, as was the glass in the windows to the left and right of the door. Simon pushed his way inside.

A blonde woman – maybe twenty-five – sat behind a gray metal desk facing the door. A cone of incense burned on a metal plate on top of a waist-high bookshelf to her right and beneath the scent of incense there was an odd vinegar smell. Behind her head was a very bad painting of Santa Monica Pier, the Ferris wheel shaped like a de-flated basketball. Her eyelids were painted blue, eyebrows plucked thin and then penciled back on again, lips the color of raw meat. Her fingernails were green but the polish was chipped off the top and the nails had grown half in new since the last time they were painted. There was a white scar that puffed out like foam on her chin. It was shaped like a check mark. There was a laptop computer on the desk, but she was typing out a form on a metallic-blue Remington Letter-Riter typewriter as the rusted bell above the door gave its choked impersonation of a ring. Then she looked up from what she was doing.

'Can I help you?'

'I need to see Posniak.'

'He's not in at the moment. I'd be happy to take a message.'

'His car's here.'

She made a tight-lipped pinch-nosed face – like she had just smelled something unpleasant, Simon perhaps – and then, after a pause, said, 'But he's stepped out.'

'Well, if he's on foot he's not far. I'll wait.'

She sighed.

'What did you say your name was?'

'I didn't.'

She gave him a deadpan, and then said, 'What is it?'

Simon hesitated, wondering what he should say, and decided on, 'Jeremy Shackleford.'

'Just a second.'

She picked up the phone and put it to her ear, whispered, cupping her hand over her mouth, looking at Simon with her hazel eyes. She hung up the phone.

'I'm so sorry,' she said. 'He's not available at the moment. But he'd be happy to schedule an appointment to talk about—'

'He's available.'

Simon walked to the door in the left wall and grabbed the knob, figuring it'd be locked and he'd have to push it in. He just hoped the thing was set loose in its frame and it wouldn't be difficult. Instead the door swung right open and Simon stepped into the office and slammed the door on the protesting secretary, who didn't get out more than 'Hey wait a—' before the swinging slab of wood silenced her. The smell of vinegar was much stronger in here, and beneath it a strange chemical stench that Simon couldn't place.

He locked the door behind him.

Adam Posniak was at his desk. A smoke-blackened spoon and a lighter and a small bag of brownish powder were on its surface. His coat was off and his left sleeve was rolled up and a rubber hose was wrapped around his bicep, one end gripped in his teeth and pulled tight. In his right hand was a syringe, his thumb on the plunger. The needle was still inches from the soft flesh on the inside of his elbow, which was dotted with scars and wounds like bad acne. One brown but blackening hole looked – to Simon's untrained eye – like it might be infected. It was a mountain of red flesh topped with an oozing brown scab. In his eagerness Posniak had already begun pressing the plunger and a few drops splashed from the end of the needle and onto the pale flesh on the inside of his arm.

Posniak let the hose fall from his mouth and set the syringe on the desk. His pale face was covered in beads of sweat. He opened the top right drawer, and simply laid his hand in it. Simon guessed, but wasn't certain, that the hand was resting upon a gun of some kind.

'I'm not a junky, Mr Shackleford.'

'Obviously.'

'I'm in constant pain. My eyes. This relieves it.'

'Ever think of Tylenol? It's a little less extreme.'

A pause. Posniak licked his lips.

'Why are you here?'

Simon reached into his pocket and pulled out his cigarettes and lighted one with a match.

'Mind if I smoke?'

Posniak pushed a glass ashtray across the desk toward

him. It was half-filled with cigarettes already, most of their filtered ends smeared with various shades of red.

Then he grabbed a handkerchief from his desk – yellowed by sweat – and dabbed at his forehead.

'Why are you here, Mr Shackleford?' he said again.

'I wanted to talk.'

'I've already informed your wife that I'm off the case.'

'That's not what I want to talk about.'

'Well, sit down,' Posniak said. 'It's your party.'

Simon sat down in the padded wooden chair that faced the desk, dragged off his cigarette, dropped ash in the tray.

'Cold in here, isn't it?' he said.

'Let's get to the point. What did you want to talk about?'

'The night you followed me to the train station.'

Posniak actually blushed.

'You know,' he said, 'research I can do – I'm actually very good at it – but when it comes to tailing people, I don't know what it is, I have never been able to do it subtly.'

'You're awful.'

'You're not here to discuss my trade, are you?'

'Tell me about Kate Wilhelm.'

'The conversation would probably go better if you told me about her. I have no idea who that is.'

'The little brunette you saw me with that night.'

'What night?'

'Monday. The night you followed me to the train station.'

'Night before last?'

'Night before last.'

'Little brunette?'

Simon nodded.

'You mean the photographer, Marlene Biskind?'

'You saw—'

'I was there. Then I followed your cab back to the house.'

'Where a little brunette was sitting on the steps waiting for me.'

Posniak shook his head.

'There was nobody on the steps.'

Simon tongued at his cheek and looked at the man, trying to figure out why he'd lie to him. If he was off the job there was no percentage in lying – or in telling the truth.

'Is it money?'

'Is what money?'

'Do you want money? Is that why you're not being honest with me?'

'Like I want you to pay for information?'

'So it is money.'

'Listen, Mr Shackleford. I'm not withholding information. I'm in pain. I want to tell you what you want to know so you'll leave and I can get back to what I was doing. I don't care about scoring a twenty off you.'

'Then tell me about the brunette.'

'I'm telling you what I know. There *was* no brunette. You got out of the cab, you walked to the steps, you paused a moment, did some strange little move with your arms like you were reaching out to grab something with both hands, and then you went into the house. You came out twenty minutes later, stood on the porch muttering to yourself – I don't know what about; listening to your conversations with yourself wasn't part of my arrangement with Mrs Shackleford; she just said she wanted to know where you were at all times – and after a while you went back inside. An hour or two later Mrs Shackleford came home and an hour or so after that you left again. You spotted me and managed to lose me by getting on the train. You came back some time later and got your car. I tried to follow you but you spotted me. It was late, I was tired, and in any case there was a transponder on your car. I figured if you wanted to lose me, fine. I'd catch up with you in the morning. I went home and went to bed. That's it. That's the whole night. Now can you please go? I've got shit to attend to.'

Simon's chest felt tight with fear, though he had no idea what he was afraid of. Was it possible he'd hallucinated—

How was he supposed to figure this out when he didn't even know which pieces of evidence were real and which were hallucinations? What if he wasn't even sitting here? What if he was in a rubber-walled room with—

'I don't believe you,' he said finally.

'I don't care.' The guy pulled his hand from his desk drawer and there was a little silver .25 in it. He laid it on his desk with a surprisingly heavy *thunk*, keeping his hand atop it. 'I have been more than patient with you. I've done my best to tell you what I know. Now I'm telling you to leave. Now.'

After a final drag Simon butted his cigarette out in the glass ashtray and got to his feet.

For a while he just drove around. He knew it was stupid. He should be on the road as little as possible – any place he could be identified was a dangerous place. But he didn't know what else to do. He was barely aware that he was driving at all – he was on automatic pilot while his mind tried to untangle this mess – and when it was over he remembered nothing of where he had gone or how he had ended up in front of the library. He had no recollection of traffic signals or other cars on the road or pedestrians or anything, but here he was parked on Grand just past Fifth Street. And he was glad.

With a stack of microfilm on the desk to his left and one roll stretched between reels on the reader before which he was sitting, Simon scanned through old newspaper archives. April or May of last year was when it would have happened. The accident. Jeremy Shackleford had been a professor and Kate Wilhelm had been his student; a late-night car accident involving both of them might have been controversial enough to get a few inches of news-print. The papers could milk it for drama – what were they doing together, this man in his mid-thirties in a position of authority and this college freshman who still lived with her father in Burbank? They could insinuate that alcohol was involved without out-and-out saying it. They could quote anonymous sources who heard such and such from their own anonymous sources. Or perhaps—

Then he found it.

A picture of the wreck was included with the news story, taken from above. The car was upside-down on top of a tree which the car had, apparently, tipped over with its weight. It was still burning when the photographer snapped his shot. The piece read:

LOS ANGELES – Famous for dangerous hairpin turns since its completion in 1924, raced upon by famous speedsters such as Steve McQueen and James Dean, and the end of the line for many who thought they could outsmart it at any speed, Mulholland Drive has claimed one more life, and pushed still another to the very edge.

Two nights ago, April 23rd, at 11:47 p.m., police responded to several reports of a car accident on Mulholland Drive, half a mile from Cahuenga, just past the Universal City Overlook. When they arrived police found a guardrail had been driven through, and on the mountainside thirty-four feet below an upended 1967 Chevy Nova lay in flames.

There were two people in the car at the time of the accident: Katherine Virginia Wilhelm, 18, a student, and Jeremy Shackleford, 33, a faculty member at Pasadena College of the Arts, where Ms Wilhelm was majoring in set design. Ms Wilhelm was pronounced dead on arrival at Cedars Sinai, and Mr Shackleford remains in a coma.

Police believe that it was burns which caused Ms Wilhelm's death but are waiting for a full autopsy. Mr Shackleford was thrown from the vehicle on impact or he would have met a similar fate.

Ms Wilhelm is believed to have been driving at the time of the accident, but police made no statements as to its cause. They are investigating 'every possibility', but have given no indication as to what those possibilities might be.

Mr Shackleford's wife, artist Samantha Kepler-Shackleford, came home from 'a dinner-date with friends' to find police and reporters waiting for her. She did not know of any plans her husband might have had to meet with Ms Wilhelm, nor was she willing to speculate as to what the nature of their relationship might be. Immediately after learning of her husband's condition, she drove to the hospital to be at his bedside.

Ms Wilhelm's father, John Wilhelm, did know of the meeting. He said Ms Wilhelm and Mr Shackleford had had an intimate relationship which Mr

Shackleford had cut off abruptly two weeks earlier. A week later Ms Wilhelm learned she was pregnant, and when Mr Shackleford 'offered to pay for the abortion, rather than do what was right,' Mr Wilhelm said, 'she flipped out. She threatened to tell his wife, and told him she was having the baby whether he liked it or not.' Mr Shackleford, according to Mr Wilhelm, called the house repeatedly to request a meeting to 'discuss the situation'. Ms Wilhelm finally agreed to meet Mr Shackleford at his home in Pasadena. What happened beyond that is known only to Mr Shackleford himself, who is unable to answer any questions. Perhaps when he regains consciousness, a more complete picture can be painted.

Ms Wilhelm was pregnant at the time of her death. She is survived by her father, John, and an older sister, Karen.

He remembered – a knock at the front door.

He walked to it, his stomach sick. Samantha was gone. She had gone out to dinner with a group of girlfriends, leaving him home alone, and left alone all he could think about was Kate. She was going to destroy his marriage. He loved his wife. They had a level of comfort with each other that he'd never felt with anyone. And now this little bitch was going to ruin it.

He'd never moved on a student. She'd come on to him. He had fucked up; he should have rejected her. And he certainly shouldn't have let it continue for a month before getting up the nerve to end it. But he did not deserve this – her refusing to have an abortion, threatening to make a formal complaint with the college, threatening to tell Samantha. He had told her he loved his wife, he had told her there was no future in what they were doing – from the very beginning he had told her those things. It wasn't his fault she hadn't taken him at his word. It wasn't his fault she'd thought she could change his mind. God*damn* her.

He grabbed the doorknob – a large reeded faux-Edwardian job that Samantha had picked up at some antique store and asked him to install – and pulled open the door. Kate was standing there looking sad. Her face was pale and the patches of skin beneath her eyes were dark. She wasn't wearing make-up. Her hair was lying flat on her head. Her clothes were wrinkled. She only looked into his eyes for brief moments before her gaze flickered away, darting around the room, lighting only momentarily on any one thing before moving on. He was shocked by how young she looked.

'Come in.'

She walked into the house and he closed the door behind her.

'Do you want something to drink?'

She shook her head.

'Sit down.'

She shook her head again and just remained there,

standing in front of the closed front door, eyes refusing to stay fixed anywhere.

'We need to figure this out,' he said.

'What's to figure out?' she said without looking at him. 'I already told you what I'm gonna do. There's nothing you can say to change my mind. I don't even know why I came here.'

Her arms were crossed in front of her. Her mouth was a hard straight line.

'But why? I told you there was no future for us – I never lied to you.'

'You never lied to me?' She looked up briefly, making eye contact, and then allowed her eyes to drop again. 'A person can lie with more than words.'

'But I *told* you—'

Her hand whipped through the air and clapped against his cheek. He tongued the corner of his mouth, felt the beginnings of beard there, and tasted blood.

'You loved me. You made me think you loved me, and then when you were done you threw me away. Left me with this.' She glanced down toward her belly.

'I never loved you,' he said. 'And I never pretended to.'

'You loved me with your body.'

'That wasn't love.'

Another slap across the face. He rubbed his cheek. His stomach and chest went tight with anger. He could feel the pink welts rising on his skin.

'Don't hit me again.'

'Or what?'

'Just don't.'

There was something defiant in her brief glance at him – defiant and angry. Her mouth twitched. Her hands formed fists. But she remained there, and she didn't swing again.

He licked his lips. 'You're eighteen. You're a college freshman. You have this child and everything you planned for your future changes. Don't you understand that? You're mad at me now, you want to get back at me now, but in a year you'll barely remember my name. You'll move on to other boyfriends, you'll finish college, and then move on to a career, and I'll just be a mistake you made when you were a kid. I'll—'

'Stop. Stop talking. I'm not a child so don't condescend to—'

'You're not a child?' A bitter laugh escaped his throat. 'That's exactly what you are. An angry child willing to throw your whole future away on a fucking tantrum.'

Her hand swung out again, clapping against his face.

He immediately swung back with his open hand, thudding against the side of her head, spinning her around.

'I told you not to fucking hit me again.'

Simon continued to scroll through newspaper archives. He was confused, and as he read, as memories came to him –

memories that were not his own – his confusion grew, as well as his sense of dread.

What kind of person had Jeremy been?

How could another man's memories be invading his mind?

He didn't want to be him any more. He didn't want to be married to Samantha or have that house in Pasadena, or any of it, not if it meant becoming this person he was becoming. And that's what it was, wasn't it? He was becoming what he had pretended to be.

Simon Johnson had lived a quiet life in which he hurt no one. He had lived a quiet life and each day had resembled the one that came before. He said hello to people and he did his job and he got too close to no one and he hurt no one because you can't hurt someone you're not close to. Simon Johnson had lived a quiet life – but as soon as Jeremy Shackleford broke into his apartment, everything had changed. Simon had killed him accidentally, but it had changed him, hadn't it? The coldness he felt over it that matched the coldness of the rest of his life – and this hot desire for something more that had begun to burn in the midst of it like a single hot ember.

And he had become a monster – he had become Jeremy Shackleford, hadn't he? Or he was becoming him – was in the process of it. All those things that had been so far below the surface of his life that they were, for the most part, mere shadows without form – all those tentacled creatures came bursting forth, all those beasts of his low life began surfacing, and they were ugly, terrible things.

He hated what he was becoming.

She spun around, lost her balance, and fell. Her face slammed hard against the jutting brass doorknob with a force that shook the walls and rattled the windows in their frames – her head hanging there for a moment despite her body going limp, sagging like an overloaded bookshelf – and then she collapsed to the floor. She did not move. She simply lay on her side on the floor with her back to him.

'Kate?'

He stood looking down at her. Then he saw a drop of blood splash against the hardwood floor. It dripped from the doorknob. The doorknob itself was covered in blood, and something meaty was hanging from it like a wet string cut from a roast. He leaned down and reached out with his hand and grabbed her shoulder. He pulled her toward him, knowing what he was going to find even before he found it. She rolled onto her back. She was staring at the ceiling with a single blank eye. The other eye was gone, the socket collapsed inward and expanded as the bone surrounding it shattered and fell like the dirt surrounding a sinkhole. Blood had flowed from the hole and coated that side of her face. Her mouth was partially open, her tongue sticking out between her white teeth. Her lips seemed exceptionally red in contrast to her colorless face, as did the blood itself. Her skin was so white. The blood was so red.

He turned and stumbled toward the kitchen and the contents of his stomach splashed into the stainless-steel basin.

Then he stood there, bent over the sink, looking at his dinner, hair hanging down in his face, beads of sweat standing out on his forehead, and a shaky moist chill still possessing him.

After a while he stood up straight and turned on the hot water and washed the mess away. Then he cupped his hands under the water, brought them to his mouth, sucked in water, gargled, and spit. He did this twice.

If he called the police, would they believe it had been an accident? They couldn't possibly believe he had planned to kill her by smashing her face against a doorknob. It was too absurd. They would have to believe it had been an accident – except that he didn't even believe that. Not completely. He knew he hadn't planned it, but there was a satisfaction in it which only increased his feeling of guilt. And hadn't murder crossed his mind? Sure, it had only been for a moment, an angry urge that he would never have acted upon – except maybe he had. Part of him believed he must have done it on purpose. And so would other people. He had recently broken things off with her, she was pregnant with his child, she had threatened to tell his wife what had been going on: despite the absurd circumstances under which she had died, no one would believe it had been an accident. It would still be third degree murder. And even if it was an accident, even if they believed the death itself was an accident, it was still manslaughter. Or involuntarily manslaughter. Something like that.

He walked back to the living room, where Kate lay on the floor. He looked at her there – dead. He licked his lips. If he killed her, he was going to prison. But if she killed herself in a way that could do the kind of damage that was done to her, that was different. And if he got badly injured in the same accident, all the better.

A sane man, for instance, wouldn't run himself off Mulholland Drive. Maybe she came here to talk to him about things. Maybe they made up. Maybe they decided to drive up to Mulholland with a picnic basket and eat sandwiches at one of the overlooks and watch the city lights twinkling in the night like stars reflected in the sea. Maybe that's exactly what happened, only maybe they misjudged a turn and went over the edge.

He nodded to himself. Why not? People died in car accidents all the time, and there was no telling what kind of damage an accident could do. Accidents were unpredictable. That's why they called them accidents.

But if that was how it was to happen, he had to get her in the car and over the edge fast. Coroners had ways of finding out time of death – rigidity of body and such – and he needed the car accident to be in the right time-frame.

He grabbed her by an arm and a leg and dragged her

away from the closed door. Then he stepped out into the spring night, bloodying his hand in the process of opening the door. The air was cool and fresh-smelling after recent rain. No one was around. It was late and this was a neighborhood that went to bed early. Her car was across the street. He couldn't imagine carrying her body all that distance in the open air; he would pull the car into the garage, load her body into it, and leave.

He went back inside and washed the blood off his hand. Then dug through her purse for her keys, found them, and pulled her car into the cave-dark garage. Then he went back to the living room. There she was, part of her face caved in. His stomach went sour, and he had to swallow back bile, which burned in his throat.

He walked over to the body, sat on his haunches, scooped one arm under the backs of her knees – she was still warm – and the other under an armpit and her neck, and then lifted. She was small, but a hundred pounds and change was still a lot of weight, and a muscle in his back spasmed, and he almost fell. He stumbled as he stood. Then finally he managed to gain his balance. He carried her to the garage, struggled to get the door open and the passenger's seat forward, and forced her body into the backseat like oversized luggage.

With that done, he went back to the living room, cleaned the blood off the floor and the doorknob – using his thumbnail to scrape between the reedings – and walked the bloody paper towels to his neighbor's trash bin five houses down.

Then he packed a picnic. He made turkey sandwiches with pesto and put pickles and olives into plastic bags. He sliced apples. He put a bottle of wine and a corkscrew into the basket with the food. They'd just gone up to Mulholland to share an evening together, to sip wine and eat sandwiches and talk.

He grabbed the picnic basket and carried it out to the garage.

He got into the car and pulled it out into the street and he was on his way.

It was almost eleven by the time he reached Mulholland Drive. The gray cratered moon hung over him and as he rounded certain bends he could see the sea of the city spread out below him. On one side a dirt wall lined with pink-flowered bougainvillea and brown rock and weeds and shrubbery, on the other a steep drop blocked occasionally by guardrails or chain-link fence, sometimes not blocked by anything. It made you woozy to see that long drop as your car rounded a bend, to see the ground forty or fifty feet below and know your car tires were only an arm's length from the edge. He drove past various overlooks – dirt sections on the edge of the road lined with wood fencing, designed so you could park your car and gaze out at the city below. He drove past houses built into the cliffside, past pink-berried trees growing on the drop, past a few parked cars.

When he got to the Universal City Overlook, he pulled the car to the side of the road, tires throwing gravel off the edge of the cliff.

He was really going to do this.

He got out of the car, fought with Kate's corpse, put it into the driver's seat and buckled it in. It looked surreal sitting there. It looked waxy and fake. Blood dripped from her eye socket and onto her clothes.

A car passed while he was standing there looking at the body, but it didn't stop; the driver didn't even glance in his direction.

He slammed the driver's side door shut and walked around to the passenger's seat.

It was harder to drive a car from the passenger's seat than you would think. Fortunately, he didn't have very far to go. He put the car into drive and swerved jerkily out onto Mulholland, gassing it with Kate's dead right leg while her head lolled on her neck and blood dripped from her caved-in eye socket and onto her lap. And then he saw the guardrail illuminated by the headlights and he realized it was actually happening. He might die. Part of him was glad of that – hoped he would die – because even if the police bought that this was an accident, Samantha would know about the affair, and he would have to face her. He didn't want to have to face her. If he died it was over.

The car smashed into the guardrail, which tore into two pieces and peeled back, creating an opening through which the car continued on its course. And then there was nothing beneath the car but air and his stomach dropped like an elevator with a cut cable. The car tilted forward and he could see the trees beneath them illuminated by the headlights. A flock of birds flew from one, frightened by the sound of the car's engine.

And then the green of the trees rushed up at him – and then there was nothing.

4

THE BREAK-IN

He read an article about the police suspecting Jeremy of foul play, another about him being arrested, another about the inconsistencies in his story, and finally one about his being released from custody, with no charges being filed against him, as there just wasn't enough evidence to take to court. He was never charged with anything. He remembered Jeremy waking after five weeks in a coma (he had slept through all of May) to a police detective standing over him – the kind of guy who wore snakeskin boots and pinky rings but sniffed his fingers to see if his hands needed washing. He remembered an inquest. He remembered the strangeness of going back to work, how people didn't look at him the same way, how he had to meet in front of several groups of people and answer questions, how several of them wanted him gone despite the fact that all charges had been dropped, how he barely managed to stay on. He remembered Samantha leaving him but coming back.

He was inextricably connected to Jeremy in some way. And now he was becoming him, becoming a man who, from the inside, he hated. He was an angry, bitter, violent man. He had a beautiful wife and a beautiful home and he wore nice clothes but he was a monster – he was a monster because he allowed the beastly thoughts that lived beneath the surface to lash out of the deep. Everyone had a low life. Not everyone let it control him.

He stood up from the microfilm reader and walked out of the library thinking about the man he'd seen in the corduroy sport coat – the man who had left the graffito on the corridor wall.

He sat in the Saab smoking a cigarette, holding it between two fingers in his shaking right hand and looking through the window at Wally's, inside which he could see Robert and Chris and a third man eating. The third man had prematurely gray hair and was wearing a brown corduroy coat. He was eating a sandwich he had pulled from a brown paper bag.

He smoked two more cigarettes before Robert and Chris and the man in the corduroy coat left. He watched the man in the coat step out of Wally's and light a cigarette of his own with a Zippo lighter before disappearing around a corner with his two friends at his side. Once they were gone Simon stepped from the car and went into the diner.

He looked around till he saw Babette. She was dropping some sandwiches off at a corner booth and gnawing away on her gum. After she'd dropped off the food she turned away from the booth and started bouncing toward the kitchen, where plates were being set out with prepared food.

Simon walked over to her and touched her arm and said, 'Can I talk to you, Babette?'

'Sure, Si—' But then she stopped when she turned to look at him. Confusion gleamed in her eyes. 'Uh.' She licked her lips. 'What – what is it?'

'Those three guys who were sitting there – ' he nodded toward a table a busboy was clearing off – 'who was the guy in the corduroy coat?'

He knew what she was going to say but he had to hear it anyway.

'Simon?' she said.

'Wrong,' he said.

Though he didn't understand what was happening, a theory was forming in the back of his mind, a theory that he'd been half-ignoring for the last three days – ever since he'd accosted Robert and asked him if he took it. This sick vertigo of repeated events had overwhelmed him again and again but he couldn't make the events make sense – not in a world where two plus two equaled four, not in a world where distance traveled could be measured by multiplying velocity by time – so he had kept them at the back of his mind. He had kept them back there waiting for something that could make them make sense. And now a theory was forming, but it wasn't whole. One thing he did know: he hated what he had become, he wanted his own life back – and there could only be one Simon Johnson living at the Filboyd Apartments.

Parked in front of the office building, waiting for the man in the brown corduroy coat to leave for the day, Simon smoked and watched his side-view mirrors. He saw three cop cars roll by, but none of the drivers so much as glanced in his direction.

His stomach ached. His liver hurt.

He pulled out his cigarettes and flipped open the top and counted how many he had left. Seven. He put the pack to his mouth, pinched one of the filters between his teeth, and dragged the box away. Six. He lighted his cigarette with a match. The smoke felt heavy in his lungs. He exhaled.

Two cigarettes later he saw the gray 1987 Volvo pull away from the curb and out into the street. He started his Saab and pulled out after the other car, making sure he stayed several car lengths back so that the man in the brown corduroy coat wouldn't see him.

After a few turns they were on Wilshire, heading west.

Simon followed from as far back as he could while still

keeping the rectangular tail lights in view. They drove right past the Filboyd Apartments, and then past the under-construction Ambassador Hotel, which would soon no longer be the Ambassador Hotel at all. They continued on. And then the man in the brown corduroy coat turned right and parked on a side street not far past a place fronted with a sign that read

ADULT BOOKS & VIDEO ARCADE

Simon slowed down and watched the guy buzz the bell and then enter the place. Then he drove to the next light, made an illegal u-turn, and headed back toward the Filboyd Apartments. If he was right, the guy would show up there soon.

When he reached the apartment building he made another illegal u-turn. There was an empty spot across the street – right in front of the Filboyd Apartments – that he wanted to pull into. He drove just past it, and backed his way in. But as he was backing in his car hit something and he heard a yelp. He braked. He looked in his rear-view mirror and both side-view mirrors but didn't see anything. The car behind him was still a good five feet from his bumper. He continued back and finished parking before he stepped from the vehicle. He walked around the back of the car and saw it – the stray dog with that ear like chewed-on steak fat and that white eye. It was dead, its head on the curb. There was blood streaked across his rear license plate. He hadn't been hallucinating. Not the dog, anyway, and if not the dog, then not Müller. But now he had caught back up with the dog's death, and so – unfortunately for the dog – had it.

'Fuck,' he said. He sat on his haunches and petted it and said, 'Boy?' just to be sure. It didn't move. Its chest neither rose nor fell. Its tongue hung limp from its partially opened mouth.

'I'm sorry,' he said.

It was very nearly dark out – the moon clearly visible and the sun making its descent – when he saw the man in the corduroy coat head around the corner – onto Wilshire – and walk to a pay phone. He picked up the phone, punched three numbers, talked for a couple minutes, and then hung up the phone in a hurry. He walked right past Simon in the Saab and pushed his way through the fingerprinted glass doors and into the Filboyd Apartments.

After the man was gone, Simon pushed his way out of the Saab and walked to the corner. Helmut Müller lay on the sidewalk across the street beneath an unlit streetlamp. He had no shoes on. Simon was fairly certain that the shoes were in the possession of a man with a neck tattoo.

He thought about walking straight up to his apartment and killing the man in the corduroy coat – he thought about doing it right now – but he needed a minute to think this through. He needed a minute to wrap his mind around what was happening, now that he was certain it was indeed happening.

He walked back to the Saab and got inside.

He lighted a cigarette, dragged deep, coughed, wiped his nose with the back of his hand. He had circled around somehow – he had become Jeremy and he'd come full circle. If he went in there, that meant what? It meant the man in the corduroy coat would kill him and put him in his bathtub; it meant he was walking into certain death – didn't it?

Maybe it didn't.

Jeremy had failed to kill him; didn't that mean that *he* stood a better chance now that he was him? Or was—

Think this through. You're Simon Johnson. Simon Johnson lives a quiet life in a small four-room apartment, working every day, listening to records and drinking whiskey every night. He hurts no one. He is harmless. He is a harmless nobody who would never hurt a soul. I am a harmless nobody who would never hurt a soul – I'm Simon Johnson.

I *was* Simon Johnson. And I could be again.

Just because Jeremy was killed when he broke into the apartment – that didn't mean that's the way it would happen this time. It didn't have to happen that way this time. He was sure it didn't.

He pushed his way out of the Saab, walked across

the sidewalk, putting his hand forward to push one of the glass doors. But just before his fingers touched that cold, translucent surface he stopped and turned away – I can't do this; I can't fucking *do* this – and got back into his car.

He opened his box of cigarettes. Last one.

He stabbed his mouth with it and made a fire. He tossed the empty pack of Camel Filters out of the window and onto the sidewalk.

I can't do this.

You have to do it.

His chest hurt and his eyes stung and his stomach felt hollow as a gourd. He looked down at his clothes – the overcoat, the green tie, the green scarf: what Shackleford had been wearing on the night of the break-in.

He laughed.

'Fuck,' he said. Was there anything he could have done that would have put him in a different position? He wasn't sure. Perhaps all paths led here. Only the scenery was different.

But it didn't have to end the same way. Just because it had happened that way once, that didn't mean it had to happen that way again.

He smoked the rest of his cigarette slowly, and when it was gone – smoked down to the filter, which he pinched between thumb and index like a joint; smoked down till he could taste the filter itself burning – he flicked it out the window.

If he killed the man in the corduroy coat, if he performed just one more brutal act, he could finish this. He could step back into his life as Simon Johnson.

He didn't care about whys any more. He just wanted it finished. And if he killed the man in the corduroy coat it could be – it could be finished. He could go back to his quiet life and pretend that none of this ever happened.

At the end of the day, he thought, it's the only sane thing to do.

Then he started laughing and he couldn't stop for a long time.

He pushed his way through the front doors and into the lobby of the Filboyd Apartments. An electricity ran through his body – and yet he felt cold.

As he walked up the stairs he reached into the inside pocket of his overcoat and pulled out the Stanley screwdriver he'd used to switch the license plates. He gripped its black and yellow handle in his fist. The plastic handle was warm from pressing against his body, but the pad of his thumb was cold against metal. As he walked up the stairs his head swam with déjà vu, with a sense that he had done this before – not once before, not twice, but dozens of times. Maybe hundreds.

But that didn't mean it had to happen the same way again. Things could change.

He felt cold.

He reached the top of the stairs and saw a graffito.

WELL, TAKE HIM

it said in black, that 's' smeared on the wall above it.

'I intend to,' he said back. 'I intend to take him.'

His voice sounded strange in the empty corridor.

He licked his lips and breathed loudly through his nose. He turned to face the length of the corridor. He blinked. He saw ice cubes spread out before him, saw his own breath on the air like a speech bubble in a comic book, saw icicles hanging from doorknobs. He blinked again and all that was gone. It didn't have to happen that way. He was so cold.

His body had remembered even if he had not.

It didn't have to happen that way again.

As he walked, a sense of vertigo swam over him and he leaned against the wall and put his forehead against the paint. It felt good. He felt sick.

He could still turn around and walk away.

No, he couldn't.

He didn't want that.

He had no life as Jeremy Shackleford.

He walked to the front door. He looked at it. It was painted white. There were dirty-finger smudges along the outside edge, by the doorknob.

He swallowed, looking at that door.

He breathed in and he breathed out, faster and faster, working himself up – making himself hyperventilate.

Okay, he thought.

He brought back his foot and then he kicked it forward.

The door swung inward and splinters of the doorjamb flew in every direction, scattering across the small living room's hardwood floor.

'I know you're here,' he said as he stepped into the apartment. 'I watched you come in.'

But as he walked in, a second wave of vertigo rolled through him and he stumbled toward the kitchen, thinking he might be sick. He dropped the screwdriver on the kitchen floor and hung his face over the sink. A sick groan squeaked from his throat, but nothing came out. He hadn't eaten anything in days. He hadn't eaten anything since Monday and today was Wednesday. He thought it was. Of course it was. Jeremy Shackleford had broken into his apartment on a Wednesday, so today had to be Wednesday. He was missing that special on UFOs. If he failed, the man in the corduroy coat would simply go to work tomorrow with a bruised neck. He would eat lunch with his friends. He would read in the paper about Helmut Müller's death.

He stood there for a long time, arms resting on the edge of the counter, just breathing in and breathing out, looking at the smooth white basin. He could smell rot like the breath of an animal coming from the garbage disposal.

He heard a noise from the bedroom – faint. The man would be coming soon. He couldn't let him find him like this. He stumbled to the fuse box and swung the gray metal door open and flipped all the switches, killing the power in the apartment. That would buy him a few minutes. It would let him get himself together. He leaned against the wall, still feeling sick. Breathing in and breathing out. Collecting himself.

Okay. He could do this. This time he wouldn't die.

It could turn out differently.

Then a sound came from the living room. He jerked and looked through the kitchen entrance. He saw a man pushing the front door shut, cutting off the forty-watt light coming in from the corridor. He was wearing green pajama bottoms and a white T-shirt.

A shiver ran through his body: that was him.

He had to do it. It didn't have to turn out the same way it had before.

He rushed the man – screwdriver forgotten on the kitchen floor – arms outstretched, and he gripped the throat. It was warm. He could feel the Adam's apple being crushed under his thumbs.

'Die, you son of a bitch,' he said, and spittle flew from his mouth.

First there was only the cold. Then the pain. A pain above his left temple like no pain he'd ever felt before. Everything was black and he couldn't figure out why. Then he did figure it out – and opened his eyes. A white out-of-focus something was hovering over his face like a ghost. He blinked several times. He had a plastic bag over his head. He exhaled and heard the plastic shift. There was a hole in the bag, a small tear shaped like a ragged z, and he could see that someone was sitting on the edge of the tub in which he was lying. That someone turned to look at him – that someone was Simon. Prematurely gray hair, glasses, a complexion like the surface of the moon. His breath caught in his throat.

He was buried in ice. He was cold. But he thought he felt open air on his left hand. He shifted his head slightly – trying not to make a sound – and saw that, yes, his left hand was lying upon the ice. He remembered pulling the hand out to see if there was a wedding ring on it. He could thank himself for freeing that hand later – once he was himself again.

The other man must have heard him because he leaned his head in and listened.

He reached out clumsily with his left hand – he was right-handed – and grabbed a handful of hair. Then he pulled back as hard as he could, gritting his teeth, and slammed the other man's head against the tile wall. The hollow sound of a *thud* filled the room and the man fell to the floor with a clacking of teeth.

He clawed his way out of the ice, groping for the man, climbing toward him, gripping for his throat.

As he fell atop the man he throttled his neck. Blood dripped from the hole in the bag covering his head, drizzled onto the other man's face and eyes and mouth. And visions and memories filled his head. Memories that belonged to Jeremy – except they were Simon's as well. In one memory of baptism he was Simon, in another he was Jeremy, but the memories were otherwise identical. Stealing the kite. Swimming at that public pool in Austin. Dozens of others, hundreds of others. And he knew. Something had happened in the car accident. What exactly he didn't know – but something. Or maybe while he was in that coma. The part of him that couldn't stand what he was broke off like a branch that was bearing too much weight. He remembered the fog that was Simon before Simon became a man: this non-existent fog. And he remembered the spells. Renting this apartment, bringing old clothes and old glasses and records here and telling Samantha he had taken them to Good Will or sold them to Amoeba Records, telling himself the same thing. He remembered creating this identity: going to Westlake and buying illegal paperwork that gave him a name and a Social Security number. And maybe he'd even planned on disappearing himself, starting anew and forgetting his ugly past, pretending he wasn't what he was, but at some point Simon became a real person. Almost. But the universe had rules and one of those rules was that ½ plus ½ could never equal two. A part of a man might break away but it was still only a part of a man. And when he became nearly whole the universe rejected this defiance, and like a scratched record this part of his life played over and over again –

because ½ plus ½ could never equal two. It could only equal one. Over and over this would play until Simon and Jeremy were one again. That was all. The universe had rules. He just hadn't understood them.

Velocity and distance.

Time.

The other man grabbed a porcelain jar from which a bamboo plant was growing. He could feel it cold and firm though he was touching nothing but the other man's throat. He could feel it because the other man could feel it. And he could see himself through the other man's eyes. As everything came to the surface he experienced both lives simultaneously. It was like two mirrors facing one another: he saw himself regressing infinitely through both pairs of eyes.

The other man swung the porcelain jar at him – and this time he knew it was coming because he was swinging it at himself and he dodged to the left and the jar failed to smash into his face. It had happened before, it had smashed into his face, dozens of times before, hundreds of times, but not this time. This time was different. This time everything was coming to the surface.

As the memories continued to invade his mind, making him whole, his vision through the other pair of eyes faded – his vision through Simon's eyes faded, went gray and out of focus and smeary at the edges. Simon had only been a small part of what he was; the part that couldn't bear the weight; that's why he had felt so hollow, so cold, so empty; and that what was he was again: a small part of him.

And then there was nothing beneath him – nothing but clothes laid out in the shape of a man: white T-shirt, green pajama bottoms, a pair of aviator-type glasses.

He was sitting alone on a cold tile floor.

He was breathing hard.

He sat there for a long time breathing through a pained throat. Eventually his heartbeat slowed to a near-normal rate and he thought he could risk standing. He got to his feet. Black dots swam before his eyes and he stumbled left, caught himself on a wall, pushed himself into a vertical position again, gained his balance.

He unwrapped the duct tape from his neck and pulled the plastic bag away.

He saw a glass of whiskey sitting on the counter and he drank it down. It burned but it felt good too. It warmed his middle.

He looked to his right and saw the bathtub full of ice. Then he looked at the medicine-cabinet mirror, the reflective film on the other side peeling away like sunburned skin. He looked at himself in the mirror – his scarred face, his dyed brown hair, his contact lenses, his green tie and scarf and expensive suit. His face was covered in blood. There was a long gash running across his flesh just above his left eyebrow where the flashlight had smashed into his head again and again. His nose was broken. He turned on the water and washed his face. He dried it with a towel.

Despite having washed his face, blood smeared onto the towel's fabric. He looked at himself again. There was still blood in his hair, drying it together in clumps. But his face was clean and nearly blood-free.

There I am, he thought.

He hadn't become anything – this was what he had always been.

EPILOGUE

He walked over to Captain Bligh's, ordered himself two Bounty Burgers, a whiskey, and two beers. He drank the first beer as soon as it arrived.

The place was dark and there was no one in the booth adjacent to his, so there was no one but the waitress to see his bruised and battered face, and he thought it'd been a long time since she'd last given a shit.

He sat and listened to the newsheads drone on the television above the bar and the chatter of old-timers on padded stools before it.

When his food arrived he ate it noisily, in great bites which he washed down with his second beer. He managed one and a half of the burgers before he was done. He leaned back, grabbed his whiskey, and downed it.

*

He slept in the apartment that night, and he slept soundly. There were no dreams. There was only darkness.

The next morning he got up and took a shower and put on a clean T-shirt and a pair of checkered pants. He put on the corduroy coat. He combed his hair. He ate breakfast at the Denny's on Wilshire and Vermont, and then got into his Saab and drove toward Pasadena.

Samantha was sitting in the living room drinking coffee when he walked in. She was wearing a pair of sweat pants and a T-shirt. Her face had no make-up on it. She looked beautiful.

'I came to say goodbye,' he said.

'What – what's happened to you?'

He scratched his cheek.

'I came to say goodbye,' he said again. 'And to say I'm sorry. I'm sorry for what I've done.'

He waited for twenty minutes at the police station before he was put into a room with a detective who was wearing snakeskin boots and pinky rings. The detective remembered him.

It was a great relief to be there. He had so many things to confess.

They put him in a cell. It was a small room with a single cot, a seatless toilet, and a sink. The bars had been painted white, but where hundreds of hands had gripped them the paint had been worn away, revealing dark metal. There were no windows. He sat silently and read the graffiti on the walls. Everything meant exactly what it appeared to mean.

The lights went out at ten o'clock.

To the darkness he spoke his final confession – his own name – but it only echoed back at him, so he did not speak it again.

Though he could not see it, he knew that outside and over him stretched the vast darkness of the universe. The faint light of distant stars and planets. The thin sliver of the fish-hook moon.

He closed his eyes.

He wanted to speak God's name, but did not know what it was.